THE SHE-WOLF OF KANTA

THE WOLVES OF KANTA SERIES: BOOK 1

MARLENA FRANK

Cover Art by: Harvest Moon Designs
https://www.facebook.com/groups/HarvestMoonDesigns

Map by: Kelley M. Frank
http://morbidsmile.com

Note: This is a work of fiction. Names, Characters, Places, and
Events are products of the author's imagination, and are used
factitiously. These are not to be construed or associated
otherwise. Any resemblance to actual locations, incidents,
organizations, or people (living or deceased) is entirely
coincidental.

EB ISBN: 978-1-955854-02-3
PB ISBN: 978-1-955854-03-0
HB ISBN: 978-1-955854-04-7
Second Edition

To Kelley,
for all your patience with me while writing this in the wee
hours of the morning, and for your help in researching all
things morbid.

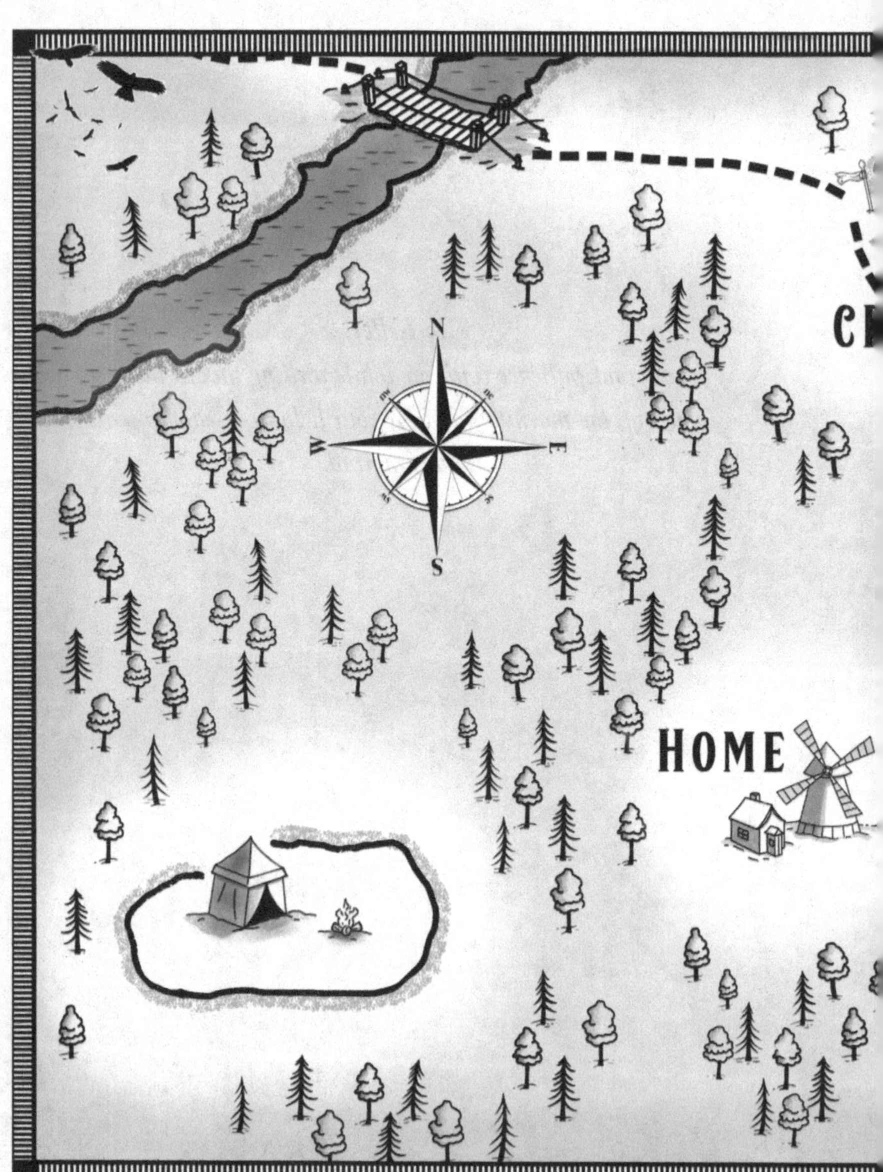

N
NE
W
E
S
SW
SE
C
HOME

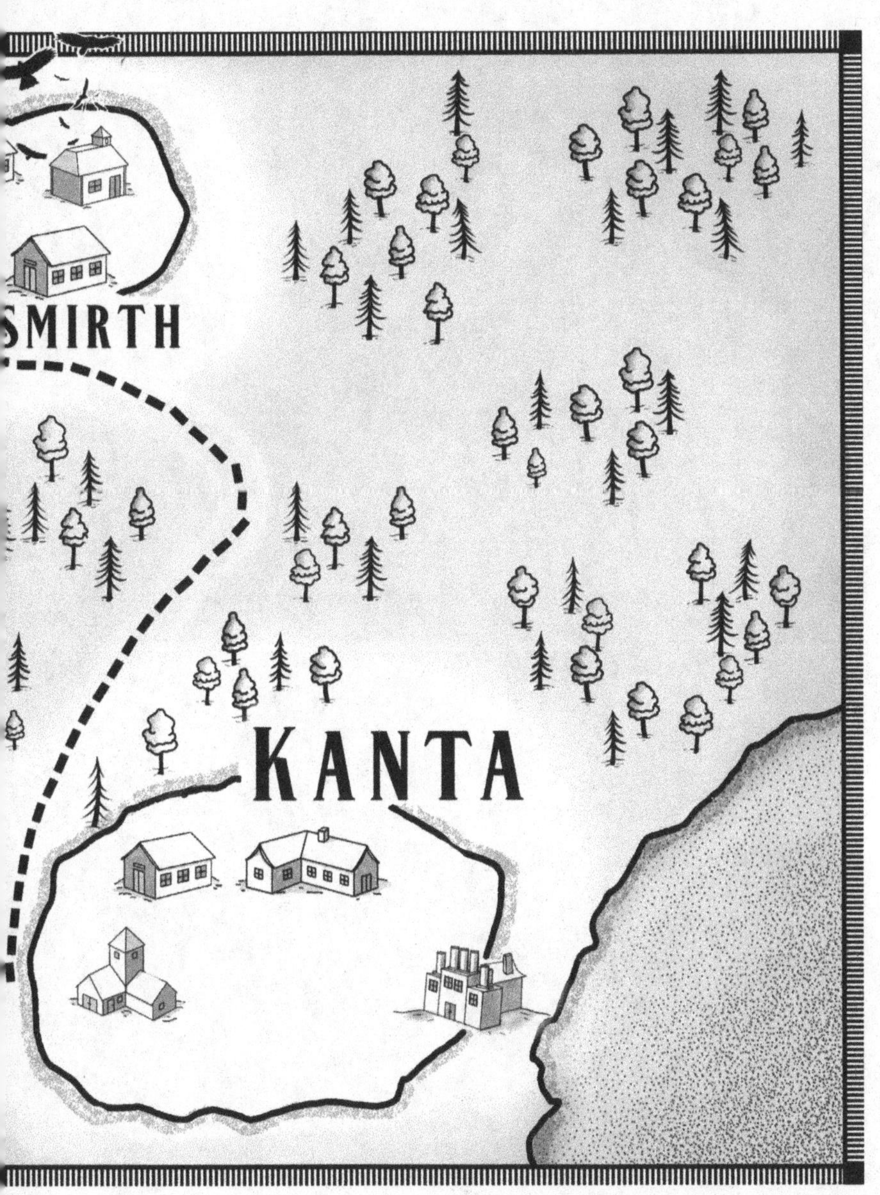

SMIRTH
KANTA

1

THE SHE-WOLF

THE CRICKETS WERE DEAFENING as moonlight streamed down through the branches. Mercy's pulse rang in her ears and her entire body was tense. Her left calf kept cramping up, but she ignored it. A moment's delay when the beast showed its face could mean a gory death. She couldn't fail tonight, not after months of practice. Behind her, she knew Father was watching, and she wondered if he felt as nervous. The forest was deceptively peaceful, but Father said they were close, and that if she remembered her training, she could hear them, too.

She got into position in the middle of the clearing with her foot poised above the pedal switch. She tried to calm her mind and focus. The clamor of crickets surrounded them, but that was merely wrapping the noises beneath. She tried to listen closer. She heard an owl in a tree, the cold wind moving through the branches, her father's raspy breaths, and the heavy, padding paws of the beast stalking her. Her mouth was dry and her body began to tremble. Father had said she would panic, that it was a normal reaction to facing one in the wild for the first time. That was the deciding moment, he had said. She needed to keep control of herself, but that was so much easier when she knew they weren't near, when she knew it was safe.

Then she saw it. Through a thick patch of bushes, a pair of yellow eyes caught the moonlight and locked on to hers. Mercy froze. It was said when you looked into a werewolf's eyes, you felt how easy it would be to become its prey. Facing one required both a strong mind and a strong body. It was as much a mind game as a physical one, and never had Mercy felt so small and insignificant. She had a very sensible and primal urge to run away. There was no way to prepare for that moment, Father had told her. That was the gamble of going trapping to begin with, whether you would be able to contain the urge to flee. She felt her legs shake but forced herself to stay rooted to the spot. If she ran, both she and her father could be torn apart.

When the werewolf lunged forward, the only thing Mercy could think of was how big it was. The careful planning she and Father had done over the past months was suddenly forgotten, and her mind went blank. When the creature leapt into the air, its arms out to its sides and its black claws extended, she went rigid with terror. All she could do was stare and gape and be fascinated by the size of it. She forgot the warnings, she forgot everything, until her father cried out behind her.

"Mercy!"

He cocked the gun and pulled her free from her trance. If he shot it, the beast was useless, and their work wasted. She slammed her heel down on the switch and jumped backward just as the beast landed. Four long black claws sliced at her back as she turned on her heel. She winced, but didn't slow down. Five seconds, Father had said. That was all the time she had before she was caged in with the beast. She locked her eyes on the branch she had put down as a marker and forced her legs to move. It was actually easier when she didn't have to look the beast in the eye. Mercy leapt at the last moment, clearing the branch. Behind her, she heard the cage hit the ground and the metal pin lock into place.

She crouched on the ground for a moment, breathing in the fallen leaves, letting her body slowly relax. That was close. Too close. She turned around to face her quarry.

The werewolf was snarling, biting at its cage, its teeth making tiny indentions in the metal. The cage always made them hunch down so they looked smaller.

She turned to her father. "I'm glad you didn't shoot."

He was standing with his rifle held out, still aiming at the frantic, caged werewolf. "You were slow."

She took a deep breath to get her body to stop shaking. "I panicked."

He nodded and finally relaxed his arms and lowered the gun. "I warned you about that." He went to the front of his truck and pulled out a long tube and a metal dart. Mercy had crafted many of them over the years from whatever metal scraps they could find. The dart's long metal tip was about three inches long, made to penetrate any part of the beast's body. He loaded the dart and walked up to the cage. The werewolf within snarled and backed away, almost as if it knew what was coming. Father held up the tube, and with a single puff of air, struck the beast in the leg. It let out a long, lonely howl and slumped to the floor. Its eyes drooped and a bit of saliva dripped down between a pair of sharp canines.

"It works fast, doesn't it?" she whispered.

"You move that slow again, you'll get worse than a few cuts on your back. You'll be dead, or worse, one of them." His blue eyes were hard as he glared at her. "I'd hate to have to hunt you down, Mercy."

She didn't look away or flinch under his gaze. "I know. It won't happen again."

He walked around the cage until he was near the beast's rear, then cursed under his breath.

"What is it?"

"It's a female. I thought for sure you would have attracted a male, but I guess you're too young for that still."

Mercy felt a pang of frustration at her father's words. She wasn't technically a woman yet, and that would hamper her usefulness as bait. Male werewolves were drawn to women, not little girls. She didn't understand why a female werewolf would come for her, though she supposed that considering how the males were preferred, there were probably more females left in the forest. Females were worth far less than males.

Father slammed the side of the cage and crouched down to eye the beast with a curl of his lip. "If I had known it was female, I wouldn't have wasted a dart on it. I should have checked first." The werewolf rolled its eyes lazily to look in his direction.

Mercy put a hand on her father's shoulder. "It's alright. Maybe we can still bring her in. Surely somebody can use her."

He sighed and got to his feet. "I doubt it, but I guess since I've already wasted the money, it couldn't hurt to try." He motioned to the leather straps hooked on to the tail end of the truck, and the ramp they would use to pull the beast into the truck bed. "Strap her up. We'll drag her worthless butt in."

Mercy nodded and set to work.

THE TRUCK RATTLED over the dirt path as branches of pine trees scraped along the sides of the vehicle. The dim headlights illuminated the overgrown road emerging out of the darkness before them as the engine puttered and the crickets roared around them. A cold breeze swept in through the open windows as the chill of autumn took hold of the night.

Mercy gripped her seat, trying not to bounce around too much and wishing she had a working strap for her seatbelt. The strips of fabric she used to tie together when she was younger were too frayed and worn to hold in a pumpkin let alone a thirteen-year-old girl.

Walking in the woods at night was always dangerous, but driving made her more nervous. The vehicle was so loud and bright that any lurking werewolf would easily be able to find them. She kept expecting them to jump out on the road or attack them from behind.

"Don't be so jumpy," he grumbled as the car dipped into a hole and back out again.

Mercy slid against the door with a grunt.

"Most are too smart to approach a moving vehicle, believe it or not."

She moved back to the middle of her seat and held on again. "I thought you said they weren't very smart."

He smirked, "They aren't, but they don't like to be run over either."

Mercy shook her head. Her father knew everything about werewolves. He had been hunting them since before she was born, but sometimes his inconsistencies nagged at her. She would lie in her cot at night and try to peel apart the truth when her father didn't make sense. She couldn't question him, that simply wasn't allowed, so instead she had to tease apart the truth when he wanted her to believe two diverging facts. Some nights she wouldn't be able to sleep because of it and instead bundled beneath her thin blanket and listened to the hum of the electric fence while her mind turned in circles.

This was one of those times. He always told her how dumb werewolves were. Sure, they were excellent hunters, but they lacked any kind of advanced intelligence they might have had when they were human. Yet they somehow knew not to approach a vehicle with two tasty humans inside. It really didn't add up, but Mercy pushed aside that nagging question and changed the subject.

"Where to now?" she asked as she stared at the darkness beyond the headlights.

"Into town. We'll see if Thomas will take her." He jutted a thumb over his shoulder.

Mercy glanced back to the werewolf in the cage, hunched down to the floor, sliding back and forth over the metal. The shot of Liquid Lead didn't seem to calm her down as much as she expected it would. She seemed alert, if drowsy, and the bumpy ride was preventing her from falling asleep.

"She seems pretty awake still. Won't it be dangerous?"

He glanced at her, clenching his teeth, "Shouldn't be a problem if you brought the prod stick."

Mercy felt her stomach sink. "What?"

He growled a low, threatening sound as his dark eyes darted back to the road then locked onto her again. "I told you to bring it. Did you disobey me again?"

She hung her head, shrinking down into her seat as the truck rattled over another series of holes, the noise giving her a few minutes to figure out what to say. "I think I left it… in the shed."

"Christ." He leaned his elbow on the window as he dug his fingers into his graying hair. His knuckles blanched on the steering wheel. "If we stop for it, it'll be dawn by the time we get to Thomas."

Mercy watched his hand gripping the wheel, waiting to see what he would do, resisting the urge to flinch away from him. She knew how quick his temper could flare up and how strong he was. She couldn't believe she forgot the prongs, especially after he had specifically told her to bring them. She usually had such a good memory for details when he requested specific equipment, but she must have been so nervous about being bait that she forgot. Still, it was stupid, and she might get it worse later if he didn't strike her now. Her father could hold a grudge.

"I can get it real quick, it won't take me long."

"You'll have to get past the barricade."

"I can do that. You showed me once, remember?"

He grunted and turned down the dirt path toward their home instead of heading into town. Mercy licked her lips, determined to be quick. He pulled up about twenty feet short of the barricade and put on the squealing brake.

"Be quick."

"I will," she promised, and leaped out of the car. She had only a few minutes where the headlights illuminated her path before they went dark. Her stomach did a flip-flop, but she couldn't let fear slow her down.

2

A QUICK LEARNER

IN THE INSTANT it took her eyes to adjust to the darkness of the chilly night without the comfort of the headlights, Mercy tried not to panic. Between the truck and the barricade, she was potential prey for a hungry werewolf and she knew it. Even though her father told her that the noise of the truck kept them at bay, she didn't fully believe it. In her opinion, as long as it was dark, it was unsafe to be outside alone. She listened past the roar of the crickets and the cold wind, and heard the humming of the barricade. She used that as her anchor and followed the sound to the front gate.

The barricade surrounded the entire property, including the shed, the power house, and their home. It had been built by hand from scraps of metal and wooden posts, bits of car parts and wire wrappings that would cut through skin. It stood at an intimidating twelve feet tall, set off several yards from the tree line. It was made to repel anything that touched it, leading to the regular death of small, curious animals, but also keeping her and her father alive.

As a child, Mercy had made the mistake of touching it once, and it threw her a few yards back, making her black out for several minutes. When she woke up, she remembered crying for ages on the ground before her father came out and scolded her for going near it. She learned a valuable, if painful, lesson that day. The barricade was to be feared but treated with respect. Not one werewolf had ever breached the walls, and none ever would.

Mercy knew the trick to get past the front gate, one that she had never been taught, but she was a fast learner. She saw her father use it once and studied the gate until she was confident she could repeat it. She slid her hand between two live wires to reach the wooden trigger hidden inside. It was harder to pull it from the outside and further to reach, but Mercy was had done it before. She also knew her father was waiting for her, and she couldn't dally. She needed to grab the prongs and get out as fast as she could, to prove that she wasn't an inconvenience to her father, that she had the skills to be a werewolf hunter too. So far, she wasn't sure if she was passing his test, but she had to try.

Finally, the wooden trigger gave way, and the

door hung loose. She moved as fast as she could, careful of the live wires but desperate to get to the other side where it was safe. There was a porcelain kick stand, from an old, white vase detailed with cerulean blue, that she had to use to open the gate wider, and another on the opposite side to close it back. Once it was finally closed, she reached in and pulled the wooden trigger again.

A wave of relief swept over her as the electrical hum intensified. She was finally on the safe side of the barricade, but there was no time to congratulate herself.

She sped toward the house. It was a crude building with brick walls, a timber roof, and an iron door. The windows could have passed for a jail more than a home, but for her it was safety. She ran in the front door and grabbed the key for the shed, spotting her mother's painting over the hearth.

Mercy had never gotten to meet her mother, but she had always liked the painting. She looked kind and had a glint of mirth in her eyes, as though about to burst into laughter. Sometimes she stared at that painting and could imagine what her laugh sounded like. She liked to think her mother was happy to find out that Mercy was on the way, even though they never got to meet. Even glimpsing her briefly before heading to the shed, she felt her understanding, her compassion, and could even imagine her eyes roll at her father's behavior. It took away the tightness in her chest.

Mercy rushed to the shed in the back. It was empty now since her father had the werewolf cage, but all of his tools hung on the walls, perfectly cleaned and organized as usual. He had a wide range of tools, even for a man of his profession: a collection of modified rifles, bottles of Liquid Lead, and the box of feathers and metal pins Mercy used to make needles. It was clean because Mercy kept it clean. She kept the entire place clean to "earn her keep", as her father said it. So she knew exactly where to go to get the electric prongs. There was only one pair hanging on the wall, well used, with a handle bent at an odd angle. They were expensive.

She picked it up, careful to keep the prods at the end from touching anything. When she was outside again, she wound the prongs up until she saw the electric spark shoot between them, then shoved it into the ground. Good, they still worked, and they were properly discharged so they wouldn't hurt anybody. That was the *last* thing she wanted to have happen if her father needed them.

She ran back to the house, dropped the keys off, smiled at her mother one last time, then went to check on the power house at the top of the hill. It wasn't strictly necessary, but her father made it a rule to always check it before leaving, so Mercy adopted the rule as well. It was what gave them a safe home. It kept out not only werewolves but potential thieves. It kept them protected.

She didn't hear the creaking of the blades as she drew near despite the powerful wind up at the top, and knew something was wrong. Sure enough, when she got close enough to see the shadowy blades of the windmill hovering over her head in the darkness, the blades were still. Something long and pointy was jutted out between them. She sighed and ran inside.

Spiderwebs grazed against her ear and she wiped it away in annoyance, feeling it transfer to her arm, and proceeded to flail about in disgust. She rubbed at her skin until the feeling went away. She hated having to go into the windmill. It was always creepy, even during the day, but at night it was terrifying. Especially in the fall when the spiders came out. The only light came in from the opening at the top of the stairs that was made for maintaining the blades, but the barricade wouldn't stay electrified for long if she didn't get the blades moving again.

Gritting her teeth, she waved the prongs in front of her to knock down any stray spider webs, and began the trek upstairs. One, two, three flights up, and Mercy was panting. At the top, she could see one light on the barricade blinking at the far end of the property. The power was going out. She stepped to the edge of the opening and saw that the object obstructing the blades was a long branch, maybe six feet long. The wind must have knocked it from one of the tall pine trees right into the windmill. She gripped the edge of the archway and reached out for it with the prongs. The wind whipped around her hair and howled through the archway, almost mimicking a werewolf howl. She inched her body just a little forward, trying to make her arm longer, trying not to drop the prongs, or fall three stories to the ground.

With a grunt, she finally reached it and shoved it free with the prongs. It took a second or two before it clattered to the ground.

"Yes!" she cried.

In the distance a werewolf howled. It was definitely not the wind that time. Mercy looked off toward the darkness beyond the barricade. She needed to get back. It was never a good omen to hear a werewolf howl.

She broke out into a sweat as she descended the steps, her small triumph almost forgotten as she realized how long it had taken her to clear the jam. Her father would be mad.

Sure enough, as she ran down the hill from the windmill, she saw her father turn on his headlights. Damn.

She pumped her legs to run faster, hearing another werewolf howl in the distance. They must have found a kill somewhere. It didn't help with the chill that went down her spine. As she approached, she saw Father standing by the gate with his rifle in hand and wearing a scowl.

"What took you so long?" He undid the latch for the barricade and kicked the gate open with hardly any trouble at all. Mercy pursed her lips. How did he make it look so easy?

"I'm sorry, I ran as fast as I could," she gasped.

He grabbed the prongs from her. "Not fast enough. You hear them out there? We've got to get moving!" He pulled the gate closed with his foot, and then hit the wooden trigger with practiced ease. She watched and learned. "Quit gawking and get in."

She obeyed without protest. She knew better than to do that. Even though her instincts screamed at her that she was outside of the barricade, in the woods in the middle of the night, with werewolves howling somewhere deep in the darkness, she ignored it. She was honestly more afraid of her father than she was of werewolves sometimes.

Mercy rushed to the truck and closed her door, gripping her seat like her life depended on it and taking deep gulps of air from her race across the property. Her father didn't seem to share her fears. He walked slowly and with confidence back to the truck, even as a third werewolf howled into the night sky. Mercy shivered. He took his time sliding the prongs and his rifle between their seats and then finally climbed in himself. He locked the doors and then took the car around to get back on the road.

"You were slow. What happened?"

Mercy felt her face flush. "The blades on the windmill were stuck again. If I didn't go fix them, the barricade would have—"

He put a hand up and Mercy fell silent. She was shaking from head to toe, knowing that he didn't care about her excuses and reasons, even if they were logical ones. It made her feel helpless and furious at the same time.

"About that," he said, lowering his voice. "You knew how to open the gate."

Her stomach dropped, and she closed her eyes to keep from snapping at him. Her heart was racing and she was still breathing hard. His accusations made her grip her seat even harder. "Yes," she replied.

"How long have you known?"

"I can't believe that's what you're worried about. Don't you care about the barricade almost going down?"

"You didn't answer my question," he said, his voice louder than before. Mercy curled into her seat, turning away from him, tears stinging her eyes. She licked her lips, trying to find the right words. "I don't know, a few years I guess."

He glanced at her, "And? Where do you go?"

Her leg bounced. Her answers could lead to a

whipping later if she wasn't careful, but there was no point in lying about it. There weren't many places she could go and he knew it. She shrugged, "Nowhere, anywhere. I just wander in the woods."

A silence fell over them and Mercy wished he would get his anger out already, let him scream at her, let him smack her, anything but deal with the empty silence that filled the truck for so many minutes. Behind them, the werewolf shifted around in her cage. Did she hear her brethren howling in the night? Did she want to join them, or did she fear them?

"You don't leave during the day, do you?"

That was it, his real fear. He was afraid of her leaving, but why? What did he fear she was going to do if she left? Run away? She didn't know anybody else, and she had no idea where anything was outside of their home. This was the first time he had even allowed her to join him on the drive into town. Yet he still had to know.

The words came to her lips with the full knowledge of the rage it would put him in. "Sometimes."

He grumbled under his breath. "You don't got any sense! Your poor mother must be rolling in her grave to know that you're putting your life on the line just to wander in the damn forest like that. What the hell is in there that you even need? Nothing! You've got everything you could ever want at home. Haven't I told you that a million times? You could get hurt, you could get killed. Hell, there might be someone watching you from the trees and you wouldn't even notice. You've got to have smarts, girl!"

She pursed her lips and asked the question she dreaded. "Does this mean you won't let me be a werewolf hunter then?"

He gave a gruff sigh as the truck climbed the hill back to the main road. "I don't know. Sometimes I worry you're too much like your mother, too smart for your own good. Girls can't afford to be smart. There are worse things in Kanta than werewolves, Mercy."

She shook her head and muttered quietly to herself, "Yeah, but there are worse things here too."

Thankfully, he didn't hear her, or at least, didn't let on that he had.

She loosened her grip on the seat just as the truck jostled over a deep dip again, and she slid against the door. Maybe if she did get lost in the woods, maybe then he would actually value her instead of trying to terrify her all the time. Maybe then he would actually listen to what she had to say.

3

A LAND OF FEAR
SOLOMON

SOLOMON HATED HIS JOB. He hated the blood, he hated the danger, but most of all, he hated Kanta.

The city of Kanta was an ugly place. The more the werewolves spread across the rural communities, farmlands, tiny villages, and homesteads, the more the people of Kanta suffered. It was a place of survival. People who gave up trying to defend their homes would travel here, but it was also the destination of scavengers and thieves. The desperate struggled here, and the naïve often met with grisly ends. The werewolves were a blight, and Kanta suffocated under their endless numbers. Noblemen who lived many miles away, in towns that only heard of the troubled lands and feared of one day meeting the same fate, offered a measly price for each werewolf's head brought to them. It did little to quell their numbers. They only spread farther; every man, woman, and child who was lucky enough to survive a bite added to the wolves' numbers.

Kanta itself had once nearly been destroyed by the beasts. It had happened over a decade ago, and the town had been reduced to three community buildings: the jailhouse, the pub, and the mill. They'd been the only defensible places as the werewolves surged each night and Kanta's population dwindled. Solomon was one of a few who had survived that bleak time. Anna had still been alive then, and ironically, the world seemed more hopeful. It had been before he and Anna were wed and years before they had Mercy. They'd lived in the basement of the pub with the rats and the roaches, who hadn't seemed at all bothered by their reduced human cohabitants. Thomas Farrell was another of the survivors. He owned the mill, an inheritance from his father, but Thomas's mind had always been slightly off. That, alongside his heavy drinking, had made his supposed epiphany questionable. Each night they'd boarded up all windows, and Solomon had been one of five men to keep watch and fire shots at any wolves stupid enough to approach them. If a shot had happened to hit a fellow man, then so be it, as he had been even more foolish to be out after dark. Thomas would never shoot, but he'd watch them fire shots all through the night, nursing his alcohol as though every bottle was the last. He'd watched as the werewolves had fallen to the ground and their blood had spilled out over the dirt. The ground of Kanta had always been stained with wolf blood in those days.

After a full week of such an existence, ammunition had become scarce. There'd been talk of sending someone to a nearby city during the day, but there'd been no telling if they would make it in time before nightfall. With no gasoline for the remaining vehicles and no surviving horses, the journey would have to be on foot. That was when Thomas had pulled out a small container of liquid he'd claimed would help. He'd called it Liquid Lead and said it would turn any rampaging werewolf into a sweet pup.

Most of them had thought it was the drink talking, and the rest had been enraged at him. Why hadn't he mentioned it before? What proof did he have that it would work? When Thomas had admitted that he'd mixed the strange concoction of ingredients himself, the entire room had burst into laughter, and he'd been dismissed by all as a drunken loon. Solomon, on the other hand, had been desperate, possibly more than the others. Anna had been sick every morning, and they'd both been concerned it was morning sickness. Unlike the others, Solomon had been worried for more than his own life. He and Anna had been the only ones to sit down with Thomas and listen to his plan. The pub had belonged to Anna back then, and she'd known where to find the tools they'd need. They'd found a few long metal pipes and a box of nails on the basement shelves. They'd wrapped the nails with paper and twine, and dipped the tips in the Liquid Lead. At first they'd been terrible shots, but then that fabulous concoction was dropping were-wolves left and right. That was when he'd realized Thomas wasn't merely mad. He was a mad genius. By morning, they had gathered a pile of twenty or so unconscious werewolves, and Thomas Farrell had become a hero.

The truck hitched and coughed as they drove uphill into town. The first rays of sunlight were shining down through the trees and gave the world a sick pinkish hue. These days, Kanta looked very different. Instead of just the three piddling barri-caded buildings with tiny holes for the nightly shooting gallery, there were more than ten lively businesses, including two pubs. There were other trappers here, too, and Thomas Farrell's brilliance made sure there was plenty of competition. Thomas paid top dollar for every live werewolf brought in, and Solomon could feel the eyes on his truck as they puttered through town.

Mercy was doing better than she had been. She perked up as they drove into town and she started smiling again. She hadn't taken well to his observa-tion and truth be told, maybe he was harsh on her sometimes, but he believed in tough love. Anna might not have approved, but she wasn't around to scorn him. Mercy simply didn't understand the dangers of the world like he did. She didn't understand what it could do to a person.

He hated the idea of her living here, doing the same work he did, killing with the same chill in her veins. He wanted her to have a safe home of her own with maybe a few kids and a nice young man with brains who understood her value. He wanted her locked away somewhere so nobody could hurt her, but he had learned today that it was an impossible task. Mercy had been leaving the house, getting through the damn barricade, and getting up to who knew what in the woods. Why couldn't she simply be happy with where she was?

Solomon had never wanted a girl to begin with. They were too vulnerable, too delicate, too difficult to keep safe. He felt that more now than ever after seeing her get chased by a werewolf and then learning she knew how to get through the barricade. Girls were dangerous. He felt like the gods had spat on him twice when Anna had died and he'd been cursed with a girl on the same day. Up until now, he had managed to keep her away from town, keep her away from the vices and evil that dwelt here, but he couldn't keep her away forever. Eventually, the girl would have to come here, especially if she wanted to be a trapper like him. He had hoped that her youth would turn away the curious gazes, but these were troubled men, often little better than the beasts they hunted. More than that, Mercy was a lovely girl. She had inherited her mother's dark skin and his own blue eyes. The werewolves targeted blossoming young women, leaving Mercy as probably the youngest for miles around the city. That made her a target for more than just the wolves of the woods.

At the end of the road was Thomas's mill, a metallic monstrosity that loomed like a miniature god over the town. It belched giant plumes of steam into the air as the gears within churned. He parked his truck and stepped out; Mercy did the same, and Solomon could feel the interest building. Eyes peeked out of slotted blinds, whispers hid behind hands, and a few were even so foolish as to gaze with open greed. Solomon pulled out the prod stick from beside his seat and pushed it into Mercy's hands. The poor girl wasn't oblivious to the looks she was getting, but she couldn't realize how much her presence was like spilling fresh blood in a wolf's den in winter.

"You remember how to use one of these, right?"

She scoffed and grabbed the handle on the end, winding it quickly; the other end lit up as a spark of lightning shot between the two metal spokes. "I discharged it when I grabbed it earlier," she said with a smile. Of course she knew how to use the prongs. Was there any tool in his shed that she hadn't messed with and learned how to use? Hell, she was probably more of an expert on all of his equipment than he was.

Without dropping his cool, he nodded to the werewolf that was watching them from the back. She looked nervous, good. "She'll be finding her bite again soon, and I want you to keep her in line. Don't get squeamish on me. She cuts someone inside, Thomas will lower the price, assuming he'll be willing to take her at all."

Mercy nodded, her eyes stern as she watched the werewolf looking between the two of them. He pulled down the truck latch and started winding leather straps around the base of the werewolf's cage. Inside, the beast backed away and watched him in confusion. He pulled out an extension from under the truck bed and dragged the cage out to attach the wheels. He moved methodically, keeping his eyes on his work, even while his skin crawled.

"Morning, Solomon. I see you made an interesting catch last night."

Solomon gave a heavy sigh. He knew the voice. He turned to see Carter Flemming lurking behind him. He was a tall, scrawny man with the beady eyes of a rat, and he was eying Mercy in a way that made Solomon clench his teeth. He nodded to the man. "Carter. Not quite what I was hoping for, but she'll do I suppose."

Carter glanced down at Mercy. "I guess your

little one isn't old enough quite yet to help out in the field." Mercy glared at him. The beady-eyed man was normally far cooler in his transactions, but there was a disturbing gleam in his eyes. "Though give her a few years and you might not need to trap at all."

Solomon pulled the cage off the truck extension. The cage hit the ground hard, but the wheels were sturdy and held the weight. Inside, the werewolf yelped and scrambled, its claws scraping the metal flooring. Solomon appreciated the way Carter, too, jumped at the sound. "She's not for sale. Move along."

"No need to be so hasty, old friend." Carter had a way of hissing his words that made them sound like a curse. "In a few years you might not have much of a choice."

With a grunt, Solomon calmly walked around to his seat and pulled out his sawed-off rifle. Carter's eyes went wide. Solomon slowly proceeded to load in a fresh pair of bullets. "Is that a threat? I'm not opposed to be bringing in a corpse along with this hairy dog."

Carter backed away with his hands raised. The fool was making threats without even caring to arm himself: typical, foolish Carter.

Solomon smiled. "Give me an excuse to wipe your smirking face from this town." He had built himself a reputation over the years, one that prevented most from daring to cross him. He believed in keeping his enemies six feet under, though he had to thank Thomas's wealth and connections for keeping him out of a jail cell.

Carter had the look of a man who realized he was a few words short of the grave and turned to run into a nearby shop. The grocer who had been standing in the doorway nearly got shoved out of the way as Carter took refuge in his shop, but the man was too busy laughing to seem to care. Other onlookers chuckled too, many of them other trappers who watched from the street. Solomon wasn't fooled. Many of them were likely far better at nabbing a child than Carter—trappers that Solomon would need to keep an eye on if he wanted his daughter to remain safe. Gods, and Mercy was only thirteen. He could only imagine what it would be like in two or three years when she began to grow into a woman. He might be tempted to build an iron fortress like Thomas's mill if it wasn't so damned expensive.

Solomon holstered his sawed-off rifle on his belt; he had designed it to be easy to carry. He clamped a metal handle around the bars of the cage and used it to pull his cargo. The werewolf's cage was another of Solomon's designs and made bringing in the beasts far easier and quicker. The less time spent in Kanta to sell off one, the better. He started in through the front doors of the bleak

Farrell Mill. Mercy followed, keeping the prongs close. She was a bright child, and a good listener, too. She had her parents' wits and the prongs to keep any fool that approached her at bay. If she could stare down a she-wolf, surely she could handle a few trappers.

A GRAY-HAIRED GUARD stepped aside as Solomon dragged the cage through the iron gates. The place always reeked of oil, and the humidity inside made him instantly break out in a sweat. The guard held up a fist, and Solomon stepped aside so that the wolf could get looked over.

"You can see she was drugged," he wiped at the layer of sweat over his lip. "I'd rather not wait too long in this heat if it's all the same to you, chief."

He had a deep voice and stepped around the cage to look the wolf up and down. "It's a female."

"I know that."

"The boss isn't taking females. They don't last as long."

Solomon sighed. He knew she would be a hard sell, but he had hoped he would at least get through the front gates without being turned away.

As the guard got closer, the she-wolf got up on all fours. She stared at him with menace and bared her teeth with a snarl. "Did you drug her?"

"Of course I did. How do you think we brought her here?"

"I've got her!" Mercy cried.

She slipped the prongs through the cage bars, cranked out an arc of electricity, and zapped the werewolf in the hind leg. She let out a yelp and curled up in a corner. Mercy blinked and backed away. The guard smiled and nodded at Mercy. "Be careful with that thing, honey. Don't want you getting hurt."

"She's fine," Solomon snapped as he gripped the handles of the cage. "Can we see Thomas or not?"

"Like I told you, he's not taking females."

"He might if I ask him. Tell him Solomon Pinkerton is here."

The guard stood a bit straighter. It was good to see the nervousness his name caused, the sudden rigidity of muscles, and widening of the eyes. Fear in these lands was almost as powerful as money. Almost.

"Step into the main hall. I'll see if he's interested."

Solomon laughed. "He'll see me. He always sees me."

The guard gave a wary look over his shoulder as he departed down one of the many narrow hallways.

4

A MECHANICAL MONSTER

MERCY HAD NEVER SEEN a place as intimidating as Farrell Mill. The entire floor was solid metal as were the windowless walls. She could hear the perpetual turning of the gears that ran the mill, its workers grinding down the wheat until it was as tiny as a grain of sand. At the far end of the room was a simple wooden table with an empty chair on either side. It looked out of place here, as though it was trying to distract her from realizing she had been swallowed whole by a giant mechanical monster. The smell of death permeated the air, as if the walls had been built with corpses instead of metal. In a corner of the room was a large puddle of blood, presumably from a werewolf, but after her father had to pull out his sawed-off rifle outside, she couldn't be sure.

The she-wolf in the cage was no longer

cowering or looking like she had ever been drugged. She stood, her ears perked forward, and she began pacing back and forth in the small space that her cage provided. She looked to Mercy, to the rod in her hands, and gave a meek whimper. She knew what this place was. The beasts weren't stupid like so many trappers liked to claim. There was real fear in her eyes as Father pulled the cage to the table.

"This place feels… odd." Mercy shuddered. Odd didn't really describe it, but she couldn't put a word to the dread that seeped through her skin. It was a place that knew death well, and she steeled herself for whatever came next. Whatever happened to the she-wolf, she couldn't show fear. Father might never bring her back if she did.

"It always smells like this. Can't let it get to you. It's just a place like any other. Think of it like a butcher's shop."

Mercy pursed her lips. But werewolves weren't cattle or chickens, they were once humans, weren't they? That was completely different in her mind.

The room echoed every tiny noise, from a shuffled footstep to the clicking of the werewolf's claws on metal. Mercy felt like she was on display somehow, as though every action she took here was being watched, calibrated, and recorded. There was no way she could voice that to her father. He lived by his senses, not so much his instincts. She wasn't sure if he would believe her or even understand what she meant.

A pair of wooden doors opened, and a gaunt man appeared with his arms spread wide. He wore a crimson cape trimmed with fur as though he thought he was royalty. His dark hair hung limp around his cheeks, and his smile lacked warmth. Then she saw his eyes. She had heard that crazy Thomas Farrell had a lazy eye, one stubborn pupil that didn't obey its master, but that wasn't what made her breath catch. It was the fact that the lazy one was trained directly on her. Even as Thomas embraced her father and joked and laughed, the eye never left her. She moved to the opposite side of the cage, eager to move away from it, but the single eye followed her, like a hawk intent upon its prey.

"So this must be your daughter. I heard she had her mother's looks, but I didn't know she had an interest in trapping."

Father wiped at his lips with his sleeve. "Mercy, don't be silent, girl. Say hello."

She gave a weak curtsy; Thomas's eye followed her every move. "Nice to meet you."

Thomas smiled with teeth far too white to be human. "Let's take a look at your latest catch then." He put a full arm into the cage with the beast and Mercy gasped. Perhaps he thought the wolf was still asleep, perhaps he hadn't noticed her pacing, perhaps he was too distracted eying Mercy; either way, she had to do something. She wound the prongs, ready to strike the beast if it were necessary, but Father waved her away.

"But Dad…" she hissed through clenched teeth, but her father shook his head. The wolf wrapped two furry hands, twice the size of Father's, around Thomas's arm, then brought her long canines forward for a nefarious bite. Mercy wasn't sure what her father was planning, but if Thomas Farrell died here or was transformed into a were-wolf, she doubted there would be any reward money. She thrust the prongs through the bars and straight into the she-wolf's belly, but the teeth had already come down on Thomas. An arc of electricity went through the beast, knocking it back against the cage with a howl, but Thomas stood fast. With more strength than she thought possible of any man, he grabbed hold of the prongs and crunched the spokes into a solid ball with his hands.

Mercy stared at him in bewilderment. She didn't notice her father had come near her until he back-handed her. Pain shot through her jaw as she fell to the floor. The world tilted for a moment, and she had to squeeze her eyes shut a few times to keep from blacking out.

"Careless girl!" Father cried, then pulled back another arm, intent to finish the job. Mercy knew when a punch was coming and curled in on herself in preparation, but Thomas pulled him back with his powerful arms.

"Easy, friend. Calm down!"

"She could have killed you!"

Thomas seemed amused rather than angry. Although he was holding her father still, both eyes were fixed on her. "She didn't, though, as you can plainly see."

Father was breathing hard. "But the prongs, damn it!"

Thomas rolled his eyes. "Prongs are easy to replace, little girls not so much."

That seemed to bring her father around, and he looked down, his expression an unusual mixture of regret and shame. He turned away from her, his shoulders hunched. Mercy could feel the flares of pain in her cheek and wasn't quite sure if she could stand yet, but Thomas bent down and held out a gloved hand.

"Let me help you, child." Both of his eyes stared directly at her and a chill slithered down her spine. She put her hand in his and allowed him to help her stand. "Believe it or not, this isn't the first time I've been shocked." He smiled and rolled up one of his sleeves. Instead of skin, a shiny silver metal shone beneath. Her jaw dropped.

"You're part machine?"

Thomas chuckled. "Only my arms, dear child." He pointed to a few white scratch marks, "I do believe our furry friend caused herself more damage by lunging at me." He cocked his head to the side. "It's metal, but I built in fuses and capacitors that restart everything when they get overloaded. You're certainly not the first to zap me accidentally, so don't worry." His eyes narrowed and his voice lowered, "In fact, I think you were hurt far more than I was."

Thomas reached out to examine the bruise that was forming on her jaw, but Father grabbed her wrist and pulled her away from him. Her shoulder ached at the sudden jolt, but she didn't say a word about it. He had already struck her once, experience told her it was likely he would strike again.

"Check the wolf, not my child, Thomas. Keep your priorities straight. I'm here to sell, not talk."

Thomas sighed and reached out to cup Mercy's chin in his hand, despite her father's glare. This time she wasn't yanked away. She prepared herself for pain, but Thomas was careful not to touch the bruise. "Give it a few weeks, but it should heal well. Try to keep something cold on it if you can to get the swelling to go down." Mercy gave a short nod. Thomas glanced to Solomon, "Is the she-wolf the only ware you're selling today?"

Father narrowed his eyes. "The girl isn't for sale."

"That's a pity. I could keep her safe here, you know, as I have others."

"I'm not sure if your notion of safety is the same as mine."

Thomas let go of her, and Mercy stepped away from him. She wasn't sure what he meant about keeping people safe here, but the fact that he was interested in buying her made her bristle. Why was that even something that was discussed in this town?

Thomas turned to her father, but one eye lingered, frozen on Mercy. "I don't intend to sleep with her, if that's what concerns you. However, there are many men outside of these walls who will try. She is far more precious than any wolf you could bring me, as you well know."

"She's my girl, and I'll decide what's to become of her."

Mercy wanted to ask if she had any say in the matter, but decided it really wasn't a good time to ask.

Thomas smirked. "And beating her? What does that accomplish?" Father looked away. "You can't protect her from everything, Solomon. You don't have the resources."

There was something very satisfying about someone calling her father out for his abuse. Not that she particularly liked the creepy guy, but she had to admire his bluntness. Nobody ever called her father out, but of course, normally there was nobody around to stop him.

"And you think you can?"

"I know I can. Tell me, how many eyes were on your daughter as you came into town? How many will be waiting for you tonight when you go home to sleep?"

Mercy was reminded of the warning her father gave her for stepping outside of the barricade during the day. Were there really people who would stand out in the woods and watch for her, or was Thomas bluffing? The very thought made her skin crawl. It was terrifying to think that her father might have been right.

Father frowned and laid his hand on the gun in his holster. "Don't you dare threaten me."

"It's not a threat, friend. It's a fact. The only reason she's lasted this long is your penchant to kill anything that moves, and your desire to live as a hermit."

Father stepped in front of her and pointed at the cage. "Do you want the beast or not? That's all I want to know."

Thomas sighed and strolled over to the cage. This time he put both arms in, and although the werewolf tried to avoid his grasp, a single hand gripped around her throat, keeping her still so that he could examine her. He squeezed limbs, looked at the length of her fur, checked her privates, and even pulled her jaws open to look down her throat. Even though the she-wolf bit, clawed, and snarled at him, her fury was futile. Mercy winced at how uncomfortable and invasive it all looked.

He pulled his arms out of the cage and turned to her father with a smile. "Now what in the world am I supposed to do with a female? It's not like she can breed with the others."

"You're a creative man."

"Hmm, that I am. Thank you for pointing that out, but even I have my limits. This is a mill, my friend, one of the most productive mills in the country, and I need workers to run it. Strong workers, not weaklings that can refuse me."

Mercy was intrigued. "She can refuse you?"

He smiled. "Something like that. The drug isn't as effective on the females, as you saw. They're quicker to recover, which means it's more expensive for me. The drug has kept her from reverting back to her human form, but hasn't kept her complacent."

Father gave her a look that was supposed to dissuade her questions, but Mercy couldn't help herself.

"So she can fight back?"

Thomas smiled. "Do you know what werewolves do here, child?"

She shook her head.

"Well, since this is your first time being here, I suppose you deserve a bit of a tour."

Father shuffled his feet. "We're not trying to

delay you, Thomas. We merely want to sell the beast."

"And forbid this girl a look behind the curtain? Nonsense. She helped you catch the creature, did she not? I believe she deserves to know where the werewolves go. Besides it's a small price to pay for the shiner you gave her earlier."

Father grunted but didn't say more. Mercy had to keep from smiling.

5

THE GRINDERS

THOMAS LED them through the wooden doors and out onto a metal balcony. The air was filled with the sound of grinding metal and sodden with humidity, brought on by plumes of steam, making it difficult to breathe. Beneath them in what could have been a quarry was an enormous metal vat filled to the brim with grain. The grain was dropped in from chutes above, powered through some steam contraption in another part of the mill. Beneath the vat turned the grinder, which was always in motion, and at the very bottom of the cavern, walking slowly in a circle, was a ring of werewolves. Their necks were chained to the grinder above their heads which ground the grain down to powder. She had never seen such docile beasts before. They didn't snarl, they didn't nip, they didn't even claw at their collars. It was when she squatted down to look through the bars that she noticed something else: all were missing their arms.

"What happened to them?" she said aloud without even realizing it.

"Every werewolf that is brought in here is modified. It enables them to focus more on their work, you see."

Some were quite old and others looked very young, but all of them were forced to keep a steady pace or else get choked by the ever-moving grinder. Their eyes were glazed and listless, and although a few of them looked up to gaze at the onlookers, most didn't even notice them.

Mercy felt her heart pounding in her chest and throbbing in her ears. She clutched her knees close as she stared down at the beasts, at their missing limbs, at their blank stares. She had known the place was a working mill, but she never understood the interest in werewolves. She never knew what Thomas used them for. Father had brought back plenty of sacks of flour from the mill in the past; they were gifts from Thomas, but she hadn't known where they really came from. She hadn't realized what awaited the beasts if they got purchased. Hadn't each of them at one time been a fellow Kantan? Wasn't this far too cruel to do to people that you might have once known? The cage that held the she-wolf in the next room looked luxurious by comparison.

"Surely you keep more than these few around," Father said. There wasn't a hint of shock or remorse in his voice. She thought of his words earlier in the woods, how he would hunt her down if she was ever bitten. Surely he hadn't really meant that. He wanted her safe and protected, he said as much to her in the truck, but she had seen how he treated werewolves. To him they lost the luxury of humane treatment the moment they transformed. The thought of her father treating her the same way, of being that cold and detached from her was unsettling.

"There are other grinders of course," Thomas said. "This is just the oldest. The first one we put in, actually. You can imagine how long it took us to build it. It truly is a marvel of engineering. There were many who said I couldn't do it, that there was no way to get werewolves to work for me, but here we are!"

Mercy couldn't speak. Her mouth was too dry. Her hands were shaking. She didn't want to show how much this disturbed her. Father would never bring her back again let alone continue her training. Instead she closed her eyes and took deep breaths of the thick, cold air. Slowly she felt her heartbeat slow down and her hands shook less.

"I don't think you've seen the latest one, have you, Solomon?"

Father sighed.

"Excellent! Come now, you've nothing better to do, I'm sure. Follow me."

Mercy got to her feet, not able to look either of them in the eye. She followed a good distance behind them, especially from her father. He would notice something was wrong with her and suspect something. He was waiting for a moment of weakness, for some excuse so he could keep her locked up in the house day in and day out. She refused to give it to him, so she would press on. She hung back and tried to keep her legs from trembling. Thomas led them through several more doors and across more metal catwalks, each sector putting another grinder on display. Beneath them more and more werewolves were paraded: young, old, tall, short; but all of them emotionless and silent.

"Don't they ever sleep?" she asked after the amount of grinders felt endless.

Thomas laughed. "Whatever would they need that for? We have plenty brought in on a regular basis. Sleep would give them time to think, to recover, and that is not why we've spared their lives. The only reason they haven't been killed is because they are far more useful alive than dead."

She stared at the one mechanical arm that Thomas had exposed earlier. "Couldn't you run the grinders some other way?"

Thomas glanced behind him, both eyes locked onto her.

Her heart skipped a beat, and she looked away.

"You do like asking questions, don't you?"

"She's too smart for her own good. Quit pestering him, Mercy," Father growled.

Thomas shook his head. "There's no need to get nasty, Solomon. She's fine, I'm simply not used to a girl with such curiosity." He gave an odd smile then and added, "You haven't allowed her far from your reach, have you, old friend?"

Father didn't answer and instead seemed insulted. On the next metal catwalk, though, Thomas paused. The noise here wasn't nearly as bad as it had been at the first grinder. At the base, a ring of werewolves walked in their same circle, but these were far less passive. They snapped at the chains, snarled at the wolves near them, and kicked at anything within reach, intent on taking out their frustration on anything in sight.

"This is the latest one. Beautiful, isn't it?" Thomas said, biting his lip in glee. "I brought in the finest workers from up north to put it together using only the best equipment. And listen to that sound! She purrs more than grinds, wouldn't you say?"

"It's too bad you hired those fools up north instead of picking up folks around here," Father grumbled.

"And how many mechanics do you know of in these parts, friend? Most wouldn't know a wrench from a wench." He chuckled.

"If you offered them the ability to learn, plenty would be interested, myself included. Most of us don't want to be trappers for the rest of our lives, you know."

Thomas waved it aside. "I can't imagine anyone in Kanta being interested in such a thing. Working with gears all day instead of hunting down those ferocious beasts? They wouldn't get through a single day of training without giving me an earful of complaints. But as always, Solomon, I admire your infinite faith in your fellow man. I must work with reality, though, not faith."

Mercy was fixated on the beasts below. She had never seen so many violent werewolves in one place before. It made her think of the she-wolf. The throbbing pain in her back reminded her of how close she had come to being torn apart. If she had been a fraction of a second slower, she probably wouldn't be here. "So why can't you use females?"

"Oh yes, that was the point of coming here, wasn't it?" Thomas laughed and wandered over to her side, which only made Mercy nervous. "I tried putting a few females in at first, but they resisted. It's to be expected at the beginning, so we gave them the normal treatment. A small dose of Liquid Lead each day and removal of the arms usually takes the fight out of the males,"—he nodded down to the beasts below— "much like it will for them in time. The females were different. They stayed just as vicious and just as dangerous, regardless of how long we waited or how much Liquid Lead we gave them. Foolish me, I thought they simply needed more time. I was wrong."

Thomas walked to the edge and gripped the metal catwalk with both hands, looking down at his enslaved beasts below. His voice was hoarse when he continued, "One day, one got loose. I should have anticipated it when she began to calm down. I thought she was simply better than most. I underestimated her. She was newly acquired, but I thought the dosage we were using on her had worked. I grew arrogant. I assumed she was submitting to her fate, but she wasn't. Once every week we unchain them to look over the machinery and do regular maintenance. After a week of regular dosing and no sleep, the males are docile as kittens. Not this female, though. She had been waiting for a chance to fight back.

"They had just unchained the neck brace when she lunged and bit a man's neck out. There was blood everywhere, but I saw it as an understandable casualty. I thought she would be sated by killing him, but instead her red eyes locked onto me. That's when I knew," he glanced back to Mercy with tears in his eyes. "I knew then that I was her true target. She wasn't interested in killing just anyone, she wanted to kill *me*."

Mercy watched him, listening to the werewolves snap and growl below. "What did you do?"

He gave a nervous laugh, "Oh, I was terrified, I assure you! I don't have your father's calm head when it comes to danger, I was petrified with fear. There was clear hatred in her eyes and she knew exactly who ran the place." He gestured to the side of the basin of the grinders. "See those outcroppings on the edge? They're necessary for drainage when the rains come, otherwise the whole place floods. You wouldn't think even a werewolf could leap between them, they're fifteen to twenty feet apart, but she did. For her, at least in my panicked state, she jumped that distance like it was nothing. Before I realized that I needed to start running, she landed on me in a flash. I thought I was a dead man."

"Fifteen to twenty feet? I didn't think they could jump that far, especially not a female." Father grumbled looking between the ledges.

"Neither did I, friend! That day I learned a valuable lesson."

"Didn't you have a gun? Why didn't you shoot her?" Father asked.

Thomas shrugged, an uncomfortable smile on his lips, "I wish I had. I never felt comfortable with one. You know I'm a terrible shot."

Father shook his head, dismissing him completely. Of course, that's how he treated anyone who didn't carry a gun on them all the time, which was ironic since he didn't want Mercy carrying one.

"Regardless, that's how I lost these." Thomas tapped his arm. "She tore them off with her hind legs, one after the other."

"Damn fool…" Father crossed his arms. "You're lucky she didn't bite you."

Thomas smiled. "I know I am. I still to this day am surprised she didn't. She could have changed me into one of her cursed kind, but she didn't. She wanted me to remember, I suppose. To remember the day she fought back." He shook his head. "I've never had so much trouble with one of these beasts. Never in these many years."

"What did she do afterwards? Jump to her death?"

Thomas turned around with bewilderment, "Honestly, Solomon, you are a strange one! No, one of my men showed up and blew her away. What do you think I pay them for? They killed her, but it did little for my arms. I'm fortunate to have the intelligence to build new ones for myself, so in a strange way I'm grateful to her."

Father spat down over the edge toward the beasts beneath them. "Wish I'd brought back ten instead of just one. All these years I thought you cut them off yourself."

"No, my friend," Thomas said, "I assure you, I'm not that crazy."

THE WALK back to the main lobby took less time than Mercy expected. Their footsteps echoed on the metal beneath them as they crossed each catwalk, and her gaze always fell upon the creatures toiling away beneath their feet. Father had been disgusted by Thomas's story; it fueled his rage and determination to continue hunting the creatures, but it had a very different effect on Mercy.

She felt sympathy for the creatures. As soon as she saw the beasts trussed up to the giant machines, she felt sorry for them. Hadn't the she-wolf merely done to Thomas what he had done to dozens of others? Death would have been a merciful release compared to that kind of torture. At the same time, she could see the pain the memory still caused Thomas. The story brought up a flood of conflicting emotions unlike any that she had felt before, and for the first time in her life she questioned her own convictions. She had never questioned her father's motivations before. Sure, she might not like his rules or hate his temper, or he could contradict himself, or she even wished that she lived anywhere except with him, but she never questioned why there was a need to hunt and capture werewolves. Now it was different. Now she knew what happened to them after he carried them off with his truck. She knew how they were dismembered and tortured. Could she willingly assist him knowing all of this? Did she really want to be a werewolf hunter still?

In the main lobby, the captured she-wolf was lying down in a corner of her cage, but she got to her feet as they stepped into the room. Mercy looked to the puddle of congealing blood still in the corner, and her chest tightened at what the werewolf's fate would be should Thomas take her in.

"As you can see,"—Thomas's voice echoed in the arched room—"I've been a little… burned by females in the past. I would have a bit of a problem trying to put another to work. Not to mention that I can't get much work out of them anyway."

Father grunted his annoyance.

Thomas gave a wry smile. "However I'd hate to see you walk out of here without any kind of compensation for your troubles. You and I go way back, Solomon, and that kind of friendship can't be ignored." He placed a hand on Father's shoulder. "I might be able to find a home for her still, if you're willing to take a small pay cut."

"How much?"

"Well, she's in good condition overall, and she's not missing any parts—half the regular price?"

Father stepped away from Thomas's grip, "That's barely more than what I'd get for a dead one."

"True, but it's still more, isn't it? And it's better

than being out completely. It would almost cover the cost of the Liquid Lead you used on her. You really don't have many options. You could take her back into the woods and shoot her through the eyes, but then you'd be out a silver round, too. We both know those aren't cheap either. Come now, old friend, let me help you." That stray eye slowly turned toward Mercy again, and she took a step back. "You have that beautiful daughter to think of after all, and I would hate for her to want for anything."

Doubt crept into her father's face, but he was still unconvinced. Mercy found the entire exchange confusing. For someone who claimed to be so burned by female werewolves in the past, Thomas seemed awfully keen to still purchase her, even if it was at half price. What did he plan to do with her? Assuming he offered half price for every female werewolf that came through his doors, money that he would never make back again, that was an awfully large loss.

"Throw in some new prongs, and it's a deal."

Mercy blinked.

"Done!"

Father gave a heavy sigh, but held out a hand. Thomas shook it with both hands.

"Why do I always feel like you're more the animal here than any of your beasts, Thomas?"

"Oh come now, there's no need to be rude." He

snickered. "Just give me a few moments and I'll be right with you."

Mercy stared at them both in bewilderment. Her father once told her a pair of prongs could have bought half the equipment in the shack back home, that was why she had to polish the one they had and keep it wired and working. Yet Thomas threw a replacement pair into the mix without any concern whatsoever. Either he had loads of money to toss around, her father lied about the cost, or her father had forgotten how expensive they were.

There was probably something she was missing, some detail she didn't understand. She was a novice after all, an apprentice in training. Besides, if she tried to bring up the money discrepancy with her father, she would get a matching shiner for interfering, so she kept silent and didn't interrupt.

Regardless, she was relieved when Thomas left the room to get the money. She simply couldn't feel at ease with that eye following her, and she didn't want to think about what he planned for his newly acquired she-wolf.

6

———

THE FALL

FATHER'S sour mood didn't improve as the truck bounced along the dirt road. The buildings of Kanta fell away behind them as the sun climbed high into the sky. It was warmer now than it had been overnight, but daylight brought bright leaf colors of crimson and gold all around them. It was beautiful, and a part of Mercy wished she was still home so she could sneak out and enjoy them.

She turned in her seat. She could still see the plumes of steam rise from Farrell Factory. The place seemed so alien compared to the rest of Kanta, like it didn't belong alongside the squat buildings made of brick and stone or the endless forest that surrounded it.

Birds chirped throughout the dense forest as leaves filtered down from the trees. The forest had a very different feeling at night, knowing the dangers that lurked in the shadows. Despite the sunny path ahead of them and their fairly successful morning, her father was angry.

He was a hard man to read on his best day, and his temper was renowned. Some days he would sit for hours in silence simmering in a rage only he understood, and her ignorance of what perturbed him could make him lash out at her. Merely inter-rupting him meant he might snap at her, or worse, injure her. She didn't want to cross that line, but she also knew that if she remained silent, the inevitable explosion could be far worse.

She thought the meeting with Thomas had gone well. Her father seemed pleased at first, and she thought it was a successful day despite catching the she-wolf, but that didn't seem to be the case. The truck took a bend deeper into the forest and she couldn't even see Kanta any longer behind them. It was just the two of them, stuck together like always. She was the only one that could do something here, and she was always the one who had to break his silent rage. She took a deep breath and readied herself for the anger that was to come.

"At least we made some money, right?" She smiled at him, trying to keep her voice as small and kind as possible.

Father growled, "That jerk barely gave us enough to cover the drug. What a waste. We need another catch tonight, but we'll be lucky if we get one. They'll know they're down by one by now. They might even know where we nabbed her too, so we'll have to choose a different spot." He shook his head and shifted his hands on the steering wheel. "I hate doing this two nights in a row."

So he was more frustrated than outright angry. Good, that meant she had a chance to smooth this over, to fix this before it got worse. She swallowed down her nerves as the truck took another bend and dipped into several deep ditches.

"What if I was bait again? We got a response pretty quickly last night. That might make it go faster."

Father shook his head, clenching his jaw. "It's too dangerous. You almost weren't fast enough last night. I saw the claw marks on your back, you can't hide that from me."

Mercy bristled.

"Besides, I can't risk losing you. You're too precious to me."

The word precious made an anger flare up in her that she hadn't expected. It made her think of the man with the beady eyes asking if she was for sale, looking her up and down in a way that made her skin crawl. It made her think of Thomas asking to purchase her supposedly to keep her safe inside of his mill. She hadn't expected language like that from her father. He had never called her precious before, and the way he was obsessed with their meager earnings for the day made her anxious.

"But I was fast enough. That's how we caught her last night. I know I got cut, but you were fine with the risk last night. What changed?"

He glanced to her quickly with narrowed eyes. "Quiet. It's my decision to make, not yours."

That only made her fingers curl into the seat beneath her, the anger flaring up again as her mouth dropped. She was supposed to be quiet, to stay in her place, to follow his orders like nothing had changed, but things had changed. She had seen first hand why her father had refused to bring her into Kanta for so many years. She had seen the way he looked guilty for hitting her when Thomas called him out for it. She saw how things were in the world outside of their home and they weren't like that anywhere else. How did he expect her be the silent, obedient child after seeing all of that?

Normally Mercy would haven't said a word. Normally she would have nodded, lowered her gaze, and accepted her fate, but she knew better now. Even Thomas saw she had a curiosity, a desire for knowledge, an urge for a voice, and the question came to her lips from a pain deep inside that had never been let out before.

"Is it because they wanted to purchase me? Thomas said I would be worth a bunch in a few years, is that why you don't want me injured? Are you going to sell me off like you do the werewolves?"

Father stopped the truck so fast that Mercy had to catch her seat to keep from hitting the windshield. She knew in that moment that she had crossed that line, leaped over it without a care for the consequences, and instantly regretted it. A pit formed in her stomach as her father pulled his hand back. He slapped her across the cheek, hard enough that she was knocked back against the door. Her face slammed into the window and she tasted blood in her mouth as pain burst across both sides of her face.

She waited, her breath coming in shallow bursts, waiting for the next strike. She dared not look at him. She dared not give him more ammunition to use against her.

"One trip into town was all it took, wasn't it? Don't you dare disrespect me again, you hear me? You're not going to be sold to some metal-armed freak, or anyone else who thinks you're just a bit of pretty property."

She heard the rustling of the fabric and knew he was pulling his hand back again. She flattened herself against the door, trying to brace herself for the pain, kicking herself for saying anything, but at the same time glad that she had. She frequently found herself full of conflicting emotions these days when she somehow found the courage to fight against him.

Then again, this was the worst time to talk back. She should have held her tongue this time, should have waited to unleash her own outrage. Father's temper could waiver between hot and cold so fast that anything she said could easily push him over the edge.

Father didn't strike her. He never got the chance.

A bullet rang out through the trees. Mercy jumped, but Father screamed. She turned to see the window splattered with blood. Father was flung against the door of the truck, but the latch never worked right, and he fell out onto the ground outside. Terror transformed into action. She grabbed the electric prongs that Thomas had given them and scrambled over the seat cushions to peek out the door. Her father was on his back, clutching his left hand to his chest as blood seeped through his fingers like wine from a broken bottle. She dropped down beside him but stayed low.

"Are you alright?" She whispered, her voice hitched.

His eyes were wide as he looked up at her. "Get my gun, girl."

Mercy did as she was told, though she had to unsnap the leather strap that held it secure to his hip.

Another shot rang out, and she jumped before crouching lower to the ground.

"We don't want any trouble with you, Solomon."

Mercy knew the voice. It was beady-eyed Carter from town, the same man Father had threatened only a few hours ago. He stepped around the back of the truck with a long-barreled gun aimed at her father. He had a crazed smile as he stared down at them.

Mercy aimed her father's gun at Carter's head, holding it with both hands as she steadied herself. "Don't move!"

Carter hesitated for a moment then broke out into a peal of laughter. "Really? You gave your gun to a little girl, Solomon? Here I thought this would be difficult."

"Don't think I won't shoot you!" Mercy shouted, her shaky arms struggling to keep the gun straight. Her father never struggled with shooting like she did, he always shot with absolute calm and perfect aim. Why did she always have so much trouble?

The beady-eyed man took a step toward her and held his arms out. "Oh, you wouldn't do that. I bet you don't even know how to use that thing."

"Maybe I do." Mercy let out a breath. Carter tried to drop to the ground just as she pulled the trigger. The woods rang with the sound, and the kickback made her elbows and shoulders ache. But she knew she had missed. Her arms were shaking, and the gun felt awkward and slippery in her hands. Father had never really taught her how to shoot, but she had watched him for years. Carter gave a high-pitched cry and put a hand to his scalp. She could see the blood oozing out between his fingers.

"She shot me!" he cried, "I can't believe the brat shot me!"

Mercy took a step back, aiming down to shoot him again, only she backed into cold metal.

"Hand me the gun," a man behind her growled. The voice was familiar but she couldn't put a name to it.

She caught her father's gaze, and he nodded to her as he got to his feet, cradling his bloodied hand against his chest. The blood was seeping out into the fabric of his shirt too fast. She turned the gun around to hand it over her shoulder. As soon as the gun was out of her hands, Father pulled her behind him.

The man was aiming a shotgun at them, and Mercy recognized him immediately. He was the gray-haired guard from the gates of the Farrell Mill. Carter curled up against the door of the truck and put a dirty rag against his bleeding skull.

"I say we kill them both," Carter spat.

"Nonsense," the guard said. "She'll sell for a pretty penny, as long as you keep your trap shut and quit begging her to shoot you."

Carter dropped his gaze. Mercy realized what awaited her. She was a prize to be sold to the highest bidder, or to whoever could steal her away first. To these men she was like a prized cow or a purebred pony.

The guard gave a dry laugh. "Come now, you didn't really think Carter was clever enough to come up with this on his own?"

"That's a good point," Father said with a glance to Carter. "He was stupid enough to ask my girl to kill him, and he was stupid enough to approach us in town in front of everybody. He's certainly no assassin."

"Shut up!" Carter cried. "That little brat ought to be killed herself!"

Father ignored him. He held up his bleeding hand, his eyes locked on the guard. "Mind if I wrap this?"

He smiled. "Not that it'll do you any good, but sure."

Father tore off a strip of cloth from his shirt and tried to wrap it around his hand. "Mercy, help me out here. It's too slippery."

She eyed the shotgun trained on them and carefully went to his side. Father had lost a good amount of blood. It had stained more than just his shirt now and was pooling at his feet.

"When you're done whining," the guard said to Carter, "you can climb up into that truck. See what else Solomon keeps locked up. Maybe he's got something that's worth more than the girl."

Carter crawled to his feet. "Come on, Mitchell. You said to distract them. I didn't think she was really going to shoot me!"

"Get going!"

Mercy pursed her lips. She assumed they would drag her back to town, but after that, there was no telling what would happen. Father was still bleeding, too. The gunshot had gone straight through the center of his hand leaving a large hole that she could see through. He couldn't move any of his fingers on the hand and Mercy knew that he would never use that hand again. And it was his shooting hand. He needed a doctor, more than Carter did at any rate. Somehow she doubted these two would let him find one. As Carter crawled up into the truck, complaining all the while, Father gripped her wrist and squeezed. Before she could say anything, he leaned in close to her ear; his voice was barely a whisper, but the words were clear.

"Run. Find Thomas. He'll protect you. Survive for me." His voice cracked. "Mercy, I'm sorry."

For a moment she felt like she couldn't breathe. The sunlight was too bright and her pulse was beating too fast. Her hands shook as she tried to make sense of his words. He would be running with her, why did he need to tell her this? "But I can't—"

Father turned to look at her, his eyes glassy with

tears. She had never once seen him cry before. All the lines of his face seemed deeper, more worn, and suddenly she understood what he meant. An icicle stabbed into her heart and all she could see was his face and the pure affection for her, no longer shameful, no longer hidden away. She shook her head because the words wouldn't come. She didn't want to do it. She didn't want to believe it. His hand shook as he held her wrist and tears fell from his eyes. "I love you, sweetheart."

He had never uttered such affectionate words to her, even when she was little. His tears shook her to the core. She wanted to wrap her arms around him, but knew that she couldn't. Her hard, cruel father would of course choose their last moment to say what she had wanted to hear from him her entire life. He would choose now to show his true, flawed feelings for her. She put a hand over his on her wrist, wishing she knew what to say, wishing she could refuse him, but knowing deep down she had little choice. There was no way out of this that didn't end well. There was no escape without one of them…

"Step away from the girl, Solomon." The gray-haired man motioned his shotgun to the side, and Father released her wrist and did as he asked. Mercy ignored the man and kept her gaze on her father. She felt numb inside, disconnected from everything. She didn't want to look away from him. Realizing that this could be the last time she saw him alive, she didn't want to lose sight of him, she didn't want to lose him despite all the pain that he had given her over the years. She was terrified. Carter cried out something from the truck, but Mercy barely noticed. He and the guard were having some kind of argument, and then Father mouthed the word to her. "Go."

His eyes were pleading. Survive for me, he had said, but Mercy didn't know if she wanted to. She didn't even know if she could. Her legs felt rooted to the ground, just like they had at the sight of the she-wolf leaping out of the woods toward her. She didn't want to leave him alone, knowing what they would do to him.

He glanced to the guard, and this time cried out, "Go!"

Just like that morning, the sound of his voice forced her into motion. Her body went into action despite the ball that had formed in her stomach and the shakiness of her arms. She turned and ran straight for the woods without looking back. She had to get away from the road and go as deep into the forest as she could. She had to lose them first, then maybe she could circle back to town kand try to find Thomas at his mill. She had to find a way to survive.

"Catch her!" The gray-haired man screamed, and a shotgun blast made her pick up the pace.

Tears welled up in her eyes, but she blinked them away. She hoped Father was alive, but she couldn't look back and she couldn't stop. All she could do was keep running.

HER LUNGS BURNED, her legs wobbled with every step, and her arms and legs were torn bloody from the brambles, but Mercy didn't stop. She ran like a pack of werewolves was chasing her. She ran despite the pain, despite the tears, and despite the cramp in her side. She knew if she stopped, she was doomed.

She guessed a good ten minutes had passed, but she could still hear them behind her, crashing through the underbrush and stomping through piles of dried leaves. They were determined. She hated to admit it, but they were so deep in the forest now that she was completely lost. She had a basic idea of where she had been at the start, but her pursuers were persistent. She had tried to stay straight for the most part, and every time she had to detour around an impassable gully or slow down near a steep hill, she expected a bullet to hit her.

The guard dropped back first. He wasn't used to moving through the deep woods, and he didn't know how to move quickly through the trees like she did. While his work kept him inside Thomas's factory, Carter was a very different story. He might be foolish, but he was still a trapper. He kept pace with her even with the bloody head wound. Every time she took a moment to look behind her, she spotted him. She was small, nimble, and would go into the woods regularly, but she didn't run in the woods often. Carter clearly did. Based on his cries, she was pretty sure he wouldn't bring her in alive either.

"You can't run forever!" he called from behind, his voice echoing up the tall pines. "When you stop, we'll find you. There's nowhere to hide, brat!"

Mercy gave a small whimper as she panted for breath. As much as her father had mocked him, Carter was right. He made a living tracking and trapping wild animals; catching a little girl would be easy compared to trapping werewolves. She came to a steep hill littered with leaves. With only a short pause she jumped down it, holding her arms out to grab the trees on either side of her for balance. The leaves hid the wet, muddy earth below as she partly walked, partly skidded down the hill. The wet mud on her shoes only made the leaves more slippery. She lost her balance and grabbed on to a sapling to keep from skidding down the rest of the way. The pine needles dug into her palm just as her feet completely slid out from under her. She landed on the middle of her back, and her eyes went wide as the air emptied from her lungs, but still she held on to that sapling. Nausea swept over her, and she hoped she hadn't done any major damage. If she had, even if Carter did catch her, he likely wouldn't leave her alive. The throbbing from her back that came afterward meant she would have a terrible bruise there later. She tried to take in a breath, but her lungs didn't want to work. All she could do for a moment was stare up at the cloudy sky and the tops of the pines waving in the wind while her body tried to breathe again.

"Look what we have here." Carter laughed, and Mercy turned her head upward to see him, standing upside-down on top of the hill with his hands on his hips, breathing hard from the chase, and grinning from ear to ear. "Looks like you took a nasty fall."

Panic seeped into her veins. She tried to move, but her back felt rigid and refused any movement. Every time she shifted, pain shot from her shoulder down to her hip bone. She must have done something bad to herself, she realized; something felt strained or pulled. She was able to breathe again, but her back locked up with every breath. Carter laughed and pulled out his gun, twirling it in one had. Mercy felt tears form in her eyes. He snapped the gun up too fast to aim at her. Mercy gasped as tears fell down her face.

"Bang!" he shouted, and laughter bubbled out over his lips. Mercy shivered and broke out into a sweat. "Bang-bang!"

Every time he said it her heart leapt, certain that her last vision alive would be Carter's stupid grin. He was a madman, she realized, and her mind whirled with what would happen if he did get hold of her to bring her in like a prized hunted animal. Father had told her to survive, but surely he didn't intend for her to be captured. Did he really want her to live regardless of the circumstances? She thought of her father and what he wanted for her; but then she thought of what he would do in her situation. If he had been hunted to the breaking point and he knew the kind of disgusting existence that awaited him should he be captured, she knew what choice he would make. Father might have wanted her to survive, but existing as a degraded slave wasn't a life she wanted.

Carter put away the gun, still shaking with laughter. "Okay, okay, no more games. Mitchell will probably be catching up soon, so I've got to look like I want you back alive."

Mercy took a shaky breath. That meant he might try to kill her after torturing her or doing something worse to her. That was somehow even more frightening.

He eyed the hill. "Let's see here." He grabbed hold of a tree trunk and began picking his way down the slope. It would be easier for him this time since Mercy had revealed how slippery the hillside actually was and left behind safe patches to step.

She looked down the rest of the hill. She had only gone halfway down, and there were many tree trunks and saplings along her fall. After the saplings, she couldn't see what was down there. Her hand, holding on to the sapling in a death grip, was trembling. If she did fall the rest of the way, she might injure her back even worse than it already was, or fall into a creek, or maybe even a cavern, but at least Carter would have a tougher time reaching her. He was moving quickly down the hillside with practiced ease.

"Almost there, brat," he grinned, hooking his ankle around another tree and kneeling down to keep his balance. "You do make it difficult, don't you? Don't worry, things are only going to get worse from here." He had almost reached her; his hand was only a foot away from her shoulder now.

"I like making things difficult," she whispered with a smirk. She let go of the sapling and thought of her father. The look on Carter's face was priceless as she slid down the hillside.

"No, no, no—wait!"

He reached out to grab her but only got wet leaves. Gravity had already begun its work. She tried to use her feet or at least use the trees to slow her fall, but that was harder than it looked. She was able to use the first large tree trunk, but that only turned her fall sideways. She slid over a dozen or so tiny saplings that tore into her back. She had to use her right hand to keep from rolling; she didn't think her back could take that. Of course that also meant a mass of brambles that she hadn't seen, waiting beneath the cover of leaves, tore across her hand. A larger tree trunk that she couldn't avoid slammed into her side and she let out a harsh cry. Blackness seeped in around the edge of her vision, and she wondered vaguely if she had broken something. Her body went limp, and slowly gravity continued pulling her down. She barely felt the rest of the fall, but somehow landed on her stomach. The pain that erupted from her back and threaded out to her side brought tears to her eyes.

She could hear Carter's voice above: "Damn! Why would you go and do that to me? Mitchell is going to be so mad. What kind of crazy are you?"

Despite the pain, Mercy smiled. By the sound of it, he was having trouble making his way back up the hill. She hoped he fell. She could die happily here if he fell and broke his neck right in front of her. Mitchell's gruff voice wiped away the brief happiness.

"We've got to get out of here."

"What? No, you don't know how much trouble that girl has—"

"Leave her."

They spoke more, but Mercy was too far away to catch it. Then Mitchell chuckled and called down to her. "Hope you're not going anywhere anytime soon. Wouldn't want to deprive the werewolves of an easy meal!" They both laughed this time.

"Enjoy the werewolves, you little brat!" Carter called.

She swallowed down the lump in her throat and listened as they walked back into the woods, leaving her alone, battered, and lost in a forest that in mere hours would be filled with death.

7

CONFUSION

SHE LISTENED to Mitchell and Carter stomp through the leaves of the forest until she could no longer hear them. The afternoon light was already creating shadows. She closed her eyes and listened. A crow cawed overhead, the chilly wind swept through the black pines, and in the distance she heard the drumming of a woodpecker. The woods sounded so normal during the day. It was deceptive.

Mercy knew she couldn't stay here. The werewolves wouldn't come until dark, but when they did, they would descend on her with the weight of their endless hunger, especially with the scent of blood in the air. Even worse, she was facedown in the earth, and would be unaware of anything that might come near her. She at least wanted to see them coming. She used both hands to try to turn herself, but cried out as her right side flared with white-hot pain. She dropped back down onto her stomach, and the muscles in her back went taut. For minutes all she could do was hold still and wait for the pain in her side to pass, wait for her back to relax, and breathe in the earthy scent of leaves. Her head throbbed as the pain pulsed. She had never felt such extreme pain in her entire life. She barely noticed when she lost consciousness.

Mercy awoke to an ant crawling across one of her fingers. The sensation jolted her awake, and the ant scurried away as she breathed in dirt. Her body was shaking as crickets roared. The sunlight had all but abandoned her and the temperature had dropped. It wasn't cold enough to see her own breath in the twilight, but she knew the cold could be just as dangerous as the werewolves.

Dark pines crowded around her like curious, shadowy sentries. As she came more fully awake, panic gripped her; the werewolves wouldn't take long. She was covered in a sheen of sweat from her exhausted sleep which only made her more cold. Her back still throbbed, as did the pain in her side, but she knew better than to try and turn over this time. She would have to make do with what little mobility she had, even if it meant belly crawling back to Kanta. She shimmied her hips forward, mindful of her injuries, and dug her fingers into the earth to pull her body forward. The small ant walked toward her again with curiosity, then did a circle before leaving again. Even it didn't want to have anything to do with this.

Her right hand flared up as she pulled herself across the ground, but it was a surface pain from all the brambles, nothing like the deep internal pain she felt in her side and down her back. Another reach, pull, and drag, and she broke out into a sweat. Her body was struggling in this awkward position and she shivered harder. She whimpered, panting into the ground as dried leaves were pushed aside by her breath. She built up the strength for the next drag.

There was no way she could sustain this. She had no idea where Kanta was let alone how far away it was, but what choice did she have? Could she hope to get anywhere in time before the werewolves found her? Did she have a chance?

She reached again, pulled, and dragged her stomach across the ground. Pebbles and leaves dug against her stomach, jabbing at her skin through her clothing. She whimpered again as tears formed in the corners of her eyes. She had only gone a few feet with this much pain. It would take forever.

"She's awake. We need to hurry if we plan to move her." A woman's voice called out from behind her.

Mercy tried to crane her neck around, but trying made her back hurt. Her heart leapt to her throat. "Who's there?" she choked out through the leaves.

The woman didn't reply, but someone else whispered something, just beyond Mercy's hearing. It was a man's voice, and instantly she thought of Mitchell and Carter. Panic welled up in her chest.

She turned her head left and right, trying to put a face to the voices. Then she spotted the lantern light. The whispering stranger held a brass lantern out from behind a copse of trees, just out of Mercy's vision. The figure had gloved hands and a thick black coat. She strained to remember what the hunters had worn when they chased her. They hadn't worn coats at all, but then again, it wasn't as cold then. Maybe it wasn't them, but someone else. She thought back to the stares she had gotten in town, the other trappers who had watched her with disturbing interest; a cold chill rattled through her.

"What do you want with me?" she asked, tears squeezing out of the corners of her eyes. She couldn't let herself cry, even if she wanted to, even if she felt the wail building up. She didn't have the luxury of crying.

A figure all swathed in black cloth approached her, blending in with the shadowy trees behind her. She moved with quick, silent footsteps across the wet leaves; her silence was alarming. She had to be a hunter, they were the only people who could move like that. Mercy's heart thudded in her chest as she panted into the earth.

"Calm down, child," the woman said in a low voice, producing something from her deep pockets. As she crouched down beside her, Mercy got a better look at her face, and couldn't help but be surprised. The only women she had seen were quite old. As fas as Mercy knew, she was the youngest woman in Kanta. Since young women were targeted by werewolves, most had fled Kanta or didn't live long enough to see their twenties. Mercy could only see the woman's eyes, but she could tell she was young, possibly even in her late teens. Then she spotted the syringe in her hands.

It was far more elaborate than the crude darts she made at home for her father to dip into his Liquid Lead, this was a long metallic cylinder with a plunger and a barrel filled with liquid. The woman was going to inject her with something, as if she were a werewolf in a cage. She thought of the werewolves she had seen at Thomas Farrell's mill, armless and snapping at each other.

"No!" Mercy cried and tried her best to move away, but her back went tight in revolt. Her head throbbed and her side ached, so all she could do was flail one arm out in the woman's direction.

"Hold still." The woman's voice was stern. She grabbed hold of Mercy's arm, held it with surprising strength, and jabbed the needle deep. Mercy jumped as the cold liquid hit her veins, then a thick weariness took hold of her. She stared up at the woman's brown eyes as cold tears streaked down her own cheeks.

"We've got to move her before they come," the woman said to her compatriot in the shadows.

"Are they close?" the man asked in a hoarse whisper.

"Too close for my comfort."

Mercy felt the woman reach beneath her and try to lift her. The pressure on her side made a foggy pain flare up, and Mercy groaned. Her body tried to curl in out of reflex to shield herself from the pain, but then her back hurt and she whimpered. The hands maneuvered around her body. When Mercy was lifted again, there was far less pain, but she fell unconscious before she could know where they were taking her.

———

MERCY DIDN'T WANT to wake. Pain moved in endless, throbbing waves through her body. Her back was rigid with it. She was also shivering from a biting cold. She heard a crow's distant caw and with a groan opened her eyes. Wooden shutters were flung open to let in an early morning light. A cool breeze swept in, but that wasn't where the cold was coming from. An empty bed sat in front of her with a nightstand beside it, but she lay facedown on a table stained by kitchen use. She was lying on her stomach with most of her body beneath layers of blankets. Cold metal buckets had been pushed up against her side, and freezing towels that had been wound into rope-like cords to lay across her back, probably to help with the pain. She shifted to see how bad the damage was, but the pain in her right side flared instead. She put a hand to her side and was surprised to feel bandages.

It didn't take long for her to recognize the architecture and familiar decor of Farrell Mill; the metal floors and the sound of grinding metal in the air were unmistakable, but it didn't answer anything. Why in the world had Thomas Farrell rescued her? More importantly, how did he even know she needed rescuing?

"Mister Farrell? She's awake, sir."

The familiar voice made her stomach go tight. Mitchell, the old guard from the woods, stood in the doorway with his arms folded and a knowing smile on his lips. He had been the one to rescue her? Had that been him with the lantern in the woods?

"Excellent, Mitchell!" She heard Thomas Farrell call from another room. "I'll be there in a moment."

She tensed and tried to move off the table, but arching her back brought on fresh pain. She couldn't move, her body was still in terrible shape, and here she was with the man who tried to kill her.

Mitchell walked toward her and clasped a gloved hand over her mouth, hard enough to hurt.

He smelled like brimstone and blood. "You say a word, and I slit your throat, child. Understood?" She stared up at him with wide eyes. Mitchell wasn't acting on Thomas's orders and he didn't want his boss to know what he had done. She hadn't expected that. What in the world was going on here? She noted the gun in his holster, smaller than the shotgun he had wielded the day before but no less dangerous, and nodded through his grip. He removed his hand from her mouth then pushed the cold buckets against her side. A shiver rippled through her entire body.

"Stay against them," he said with a flat gaze. He looked like he wanted her dead, but if that was the case, why was he trying to heal the wounds that he had helped cause?

She nodded again, not quite sure what was safe to say. He pulled out towels and started replacing the wet ones around the metal buckets. Then he took the wet towels to the window and began wringing them out over the edge. "She certainly doesn't seem happy," he said loud enough for Thomas to hear him, glancing back to her with flat eyes that didn't match the humor in his voice.

"I would think not, after what she's been through!"

She watched Mitchell move through the pile of wet towels, wringing them out one by one over the edge of the balcony, her brain foggy and slow to catch up on what this all meant. Thomas had rescued her from the werewolves, but the real threat was right here under his roof. She wasn't sure which was worse, being torn apart by werewolves or imprisoned with a man who had tried to kill her.

Thomas stepped in with a heavy sigh. His red hair was askew and he no longer wore his red cape, but instead a simple black outfit. "Oh you silly, foolish girl." He put a pitcher of water down on the nightstand, then sat down on the empty bed. "Though I suppose you're not really to blame. You can't help who you were born to. Solomon was stubborn, even to the end, I understand." He shook his head.

"Is he dead?" Her voice cracked at the first words she had spoken.

Thomas nodded, and a wave of guilt and sadness swept through her. Some small part of her had been hoping that her father was still alive, but that hope was squashed like a firefly underfoot. He had told her to survive because he knew that he wouldn't.

A pained look came over Thomas's face as he poured her a glass of water. Both his good eye and his lazy one were aimed at her, and it made her nervous that Mitchell was standing behind him at the window. She glanced to him, unable to refrain from shaking with the anger that filled her. Mitchell was probably the one who'd pulled the trigger.

Carter chased after her and he had been in the truck bed. That meant Mitchell was the one who stayed behind to kill him. Just looking at him made the pit of sadness that wanted to tear her apart shift into a boiling rage.

Thomas had to help her lean up so she could drink, but the ice had helped keep the swelling down, and that made it easier to move. She was surprised at how thirsty she felt, but took her time drinking so she could think. She needed to find out why Thomas had saved her, but without outing Mitchell. She couldn't mention anything incriminating about Mitchell, not while he was in the room, but she needed to find out how much Thomas knew. She needed to determine if he was an innocent in all of this or if he was equally to blame. After he laid her back down again she asked, "Did you send them to kill my father?"

She kept her gaze on Thomas, but in her peripheral vision she caught Mitchell freeze at the window and turn to look at them.

Thomas sighed and shook his head. "Why in the world would you think such a thing?"

She swallowed hard, trying to choose the right words. "You wanted me here with you. That's what you told my father at least, and now I guess you have me, just like the she-wolf. Seems like you got exactly what you wanted."

The gaunt man studied her with a mixture of

disgust and concern. "You're just as distrustful and suspicious as your father was, you know that? You're lucky to be alive."

"Do you mean I owe you something?"

Thomas blinked. "What?"

"In exchange for my life."

He chuckled and gave a wide smile, then promptly avoided the question. "We're not sure who attacked you two, but we did find your father's body." His smile fell, and he swallowed before continuing. "Did you see their faces? Now I know that you're not familiar with most of the people in this town, but I must implore you to think carefully when I ask you this: did you see who they were? Even if you don't know their names, just a description of their clothes or their faces would help."

The breath caught in her throat, and her fingers gripped the blanket. She wanted to aim a finger at Mitchell's head. She wished she didn't care if she lived or died; she wished that vengeance alone was her sole wish in life, but Father's words came back to her like the tolling of a bell: Survive for me. She closed her eyes. Couldn't he have asked for something easier? Kill them all, Mercy—she could have maybe managed that.

When she opened her eyes again, Thomas was watching her closely. He looked at her so intently that it sent a shiver through her. It took an act of will not to look at Mitchell, not to out him as possibly the ringleader for the attack. In her peripheral vision he stood with his legs apart, his hands at his side, and she knew that he could shoot to kill them both in an instant if she said the wrong words. She took a deep breath and looked down, shaking her head.

"You're certain of that? You seem like a bright child, Mercy, not one who would miss such an important detail."

She took another deep breath to calm her rage, to ease her aching fury. "I'm sorry," she whispered. "I guess I was just frightened."

"That's a pity." Thomas sighed and sat back, his gaze distant. It seemed like he truly had hoped she could help find her father's murderers. And she certainly wished she could. "Years ago this town was rife with young women, though I'm sure it's hard to believe now. We even had our own whorehouse." He chuckled. "Then unfortunately women became one of our top exports for a few years. Do you know how many attacked you two? Solomon had made a number of enemies for himself, I understand. Were any of them trappers?"

She had to force her jaw to unclench as an opening appeared. She looked Thomas in the eyes. "Yes, one of them was."

She heard Mitchell drop one of the wet towels to the ground.

"But not one you recognized," Thomas pushed.

She shook her head again.

Thomas breathed out through his nose, watching her closely, as though he could see her lies. Mercy forced her face to be as empty of emotion as possible, trying her best not to get them both killed. "Quite a pity. Did you know that there are hunters in this town who have never once brought a were-wolf to me? Not once in the many years that I've offered my services."

She looked up at him. "Why does that matter? Perhaps they're just not very good."

Thomas smirked. "Their prey is not the were-wolf, but rather the people who live here. I suspect they've stolen away several children in this town, and simply declared them lost to werewolf attacks." He winked his good eye at her shocked expression. "I may seem like I have little interest in this little spit of a town, but I do appreciate it. This is my home, too. I would sleep better at night if I could put away those responsible for your father's death."

Mercy cleared her throat, well aware of Mitchell's intense gaze on her. "Thank you for rescuing me, but I would like to know why."

Thomas gave a tight smile. "That's a very good question. To be honest, I'm not entirely sure myself. Maybe I thought you would be quite lovely in a few years and I hate to see beauty wasted."

She didn't believe him. Despite his smirk, there was a quality to his features that didn't match the greed that she had seen in the trappers as she and her father walked through town earlier. He was lying, but of course, so was she. Perhaps that wasn't quite the question she needed to ask. She changed directions. "I'm flattered, but I don't believe you. To be honest with you, Mr. Farrell, I don't like the idea of owing a life debt to someone and not knowing how I'll be repaying it. Especially when you give me comments like that."

Thomas winced and arched his eyebrows. "You have quite the fiery tongue for your sex, do you know that?"

Mercy didn't take his bait. She locked eyes with him and waited. Despite the fact that she was injured and far younger than him, Thomas shifted beneath her gaze; it made her feel powerful. She wondered if this was how her father felt when he made men squirm. She could understand the appeal.

With a huff, Thomas got to his feet. "As you know, I indulge in many tastes, dear girl. I have my curiosities, my hobbies you might say, and my hunches. Right now, I think you will be far more useful to me alive than as a carcass in the woods being devoured by werewolves."

It was Mercy's turn to wince.

"I have a few ideas in mind, but I think it's best for you to focus on your health first. I need you to recover." He walked to the doorway and gestured for Mitchell to join him in the hall without a glance back to her. Mitchell followed him, but not before tossing a glare in her direction.

Mercy took a shaky breath and gave a ragged cough that hurt her chest. She brought an arm up and awkwardly rubbed at her eyes as she allowed the tension to unwind from her body. She hoped she hadn't destroyed her chances by challenging Thomas like that. The discussion had gone from bemused banter to terse annoyance in just a few moments. She had gotten so wrapped up in playing the game, trying her best to be her father, that she had forgotten that she was in Thomas's home now. She had forgotten that she was completely at his mercy and that if she did recover, it would be because of his generosity. Thomas could have had her killed at any time if he wanted and no one would care. Her father was her only family left and anyone else in Kanta that was interested in her wanted her merely as a product, not for who she was. She couldn't help but wonder at what Thomas alluded to regarding her usefulness.

What she wouldn't give to hear her father once more, to hand this whole mess over to him to solve, to hear him answer questions in plain language and not dodge or dance to another topic every other sentence. Dealing with Thomas was exhausting. It was honestly no wonder her father always had such a short temper with him when he visited the man.

She had once thought her father simple because his terse, direct comments, but now she appreciated it for what it was: brutal honesty.

She sank down under the blankets, and somehow, despite the shivering, fell asleep out of pure exhaustion.

8

THE LIFE DEBT

EVEN IN HER dreams the mill continued to grind. It was a constant sound, just like the footsteps of those werewolves she had seen harnessed. Sometimes she imagined she could hear them biting and snapping at each other, other times she heard them howl into the sky. In one fitful dream she leaped from the bed and ran to the window and saw the werewolves watching her as they walked in circles around the grinder. Their gazes were locked onto her and their eyes shone yellow in the darkness. It was terrifying.

All throughout her nightmares and feverish dreams, the grinder continued, bleeding between the gaps of sleep and wakefulness, stitching everything together so that it felt like an endless dream she couldn't wake from.

A sharp pinprick on her arm made her entire

body snap to attention. She opened her eyes with a jolt as she tried to make sense of what was happening to her. Was it another dream or was it real? She looked down to see a needle jabbed into her forearm.

It was Mitchell. It had to be. He finally found a way to get rid of her for good while she slept. What was he giving her? Poison? Liquid Lead like the werewolves below? She reached down to pull it out, but her fingers were slippery. She kept missing. Finally when she wrapped her hand around the needle, a hand wrapped around her wrist, holding her steady.

She whimpered and tried to pull away, but they wouldn't let go. She glanced up to see it wasn't Mitchell drugging her, but a man who was mostly bald with wispy white hair and furrowed eyebrows. She was familiar somehow. She had seen him before, but it was years ago.

Dr. Keene, that's who it was. He had visited her home before, years ago when Father had hurt himself in the woods. It was while he was repairing the barricade. He was trying to get metal wire to wrap around a fence post, but it sprang back and sliced up his forearm. Blood dripped down his arm in rivulets and his scream made a flock of crows fly into the sky.

She couldn't remember how Dr. Keene had known to come, but he showed up with his black leather bag and a deep frown. Father was supposed to rest for a week, but he still insisted on walking Mercy through how to fix the fence instead. She remembered wrapping the metal wire with shaky fingers, afraid her arm would get sliced open next.

Dr. Keene was older now, but his pale eyes were the same. He had a warmth to him that she couldn't describe, a presence that calmed her even though she was in this strange place. He put a cool cloth to her forehead, and she relaxed into the pillow in a confused haze.

"Get rid of those buckets first of all. She needs rest, and you'll likely give her hypothermia instead. Muscles can heal, but she'll never fight this sickness off in her current state."

The liquid in her wrist spread warmth through her body, forcing her eyes to close even though she wanted to know what was happening to her. Her body went as limp as a doll.

She flopped her head to the side and forced her eyes open once more. There in the doorway stood Mitchell, waiting like a spider in the shadows, ever the patient assassin. She saw no emotion on his face, just that same insufferable emotionless mask with his hands clasped behind his back.

What would happen to her if she was forced to sleep again? What if this time he truly meant to kill her? A jolt of panic made her legs twitch and she tried to sit up, reaching a hand out to the edge of the bed, intent on pulling herself up, but Dr. Keene put a hand on her shoulder and gently pushed her back down.

"Easy there, it's okay. You need to rest. Just close your eyes and sleep, child."

She glanced at him, her body sluggish and her tongue too big to speak.

"He's going to—" It was too difficult to talk, too exhausting, each word felt like it took too much effort.

He rested a warm hand on her cheek.

"There, there, it's going to be alright. No one's going to get you." He gave her a weak smile, as though he didn't fully believe his own words.

How many young women had he treated in Kanta? How could he say such a thing when he knew very well that this wasn't her home? She wanted to ask him so many questions but she was afraid of knowing what he would say.

She was terrified of falling asleep, but unable to fight the drug. She tried to say more, but her body refused to fight any longer. All she could do was whimper as sleep gathered around her, pulling her into a darkness without dreams, without pain, and without protection.

IT WAS night when Mercy finally awoke.

Crickets from the woods were loud enough that she could hear them from her room beyond the monotonous grinding of the mill. Her windows were cracked open and she could smell rain in the air. It was unusually warm for autumn, and the humidity from the grinders made the sheets stick to her skin.

She had no idea if it was the same night or if she had slept for days. Time no longer belonged to her.

At some point she had been pushed onto her side; she hoped it had been Dr. Keene. Then again, she wasn't sure if even he was trustworthy anymore. She remembered how frightened she had been seeing Mitchell standing in the doorway and was a little surprised that he had let her heal. She had expected him to use her weakness to take her out, to kill the one person who knew his secret.

But he hadn't tried to kill her. Instead he was the one who played nursemaid so she could regain her health. What was he planning? Why did he want her well? Or was that part of the plan so that she would fetch top dollar to whoever he planned to sell her to? She shuddered.

Her side ached, but her back felt much better than it had, save for the usual stiffness from lying down for too long. Her throat was also a little sore, but she wasn't coughing like she had been. Dr.

Keene had mentioned a sickness, had she recovered from that as well?

With slow, cautious movements she pushed herself up to a sitting position. Her ribs throbbed in protest as did her skull. She focused on the oil lamp on the nightstand, on the calm flame that burned within the grimy hurricane glass. A warm breeze drifted in through the windows as the first patter of rain began to hit the glass and the wooden floorboards.

She listened to the rain, focused on the random sounds of the drops. Slowly the throbbing of her ribs dimmed to a dull ache and her pounding headache diminished. She took a deep breath and caught the pungent smell of mechanical steam from the ever-spinning grinders mixing with the autumn rain.

She had been feverish when Dr. Keene had been there. Even though the sheets stuck to her due to the humidity, her hair wasn't wet with sweat. In fact, she felt freshly scrubbed, and she couldn't help the anxiety that thought brought. The thought of Mitchell bathing her made her chest tighten. Surely he wouldn't have been given such a menial task, would he? He was a guard, not a nursemaid; then again, he had tended to the wet towels before. It seemed to be his task to nurse her back to help. She swallowed down the disgust.

"What a fortunate child you are." With a gasp,

Mercy turned to the dark figure leaning in the doorway. At first glance she thought it was Mitchell, but it was a woman's voice. She had heard that voice before. It was the woman from the woods.

"You." Mercy's voice felt hollow, as though her injuries and illness had taken all the fight from her body. She cleared her throat.

The woman stepped inside with a chuckle, her footsteps silent on the metal floor. She was wrapped in black fabric from head to toe, all except her eyes. She was dressed just as she had been the night that she drugged her in the forest. A part of her had wondered if the woman had been a hallucination, especially with how bad her injuries were at the time, and seeing her now when she had just awoken from her fevered sleep made that otherworldliness still seem plausible. "Who are you?"

The woman poured two glasses of water with a carafe beside the bed, and the candlelight glinted in her eyes. Her skin was dark, far darker than Mercy's, and her eyes were like liquid caramel. Mercy drank deeply from the glass the woman handed her; the tepid water soothed her dry throat. She was surprised by her thirst.

"My name is Leyda, and I'm here to help you."

Mercy's heart soared at the idea. She needed a savior, she wanted one so badly, but her father had taught her to be a pragmatist. If he had taught her anything, it was that there was nothing given freely in this world. Everyone wanted something in exchange.

"With every step of recovery," Leyda said, "you put yourself in more danger."

"What do you mean?"

Leyda put a hand out and touched a bit of Mercy's hair. "You must be tired of it: always running away and never fighting back."

Mercy clenched her jaw. It sounded like something her father might say, and for the first time she wondered if he would have seen her actions as cowardly. But he had asked her to survive, hadn't he? Wasn't she doing exactly what he had asked of her with his final words?

Leyda's eyes crinkled in a smile. "I can help you, if you'll let me."

Mercy narrowed her eyes. As desperate as she was for a savior, she didn't trust this woman. "How do you plan to do that?"

The woman began unwrapping the fabric around her head. "By giving you an option you've not had before." Layers of fabric pulled away from her throat. "By giving you a gift." More layers pulled away from the top of her head. "By changing you." The strips of fabric were pulled away from her face, and Mercy's eyes widened.

Her face looked like a patch of muddy dirt that had been rolled over by too many vehicles. The skin was folded in odd places, tufts of fur stuck out in others. Her jaw was jutted forward almost like a wolf's snout, but her mouth was that of a human. Her pointed ears were too high up on her head to possibly be human, and it made her look like something out of a nightmare. It took Mercy a few moments to make sense of it, to piece together what the face was supposed to be and to understand why it was so contorted. Leyda smiled and the warmth and humanity of it seemed to finish the disturbing sight, to pull the pieces of the puzzle together finally so that she could see the full picture.

"You're a werewolf," Mercy whispered, trying to explain the sight to herself as much as confirm it.

"Indeed."

Mercy found herself leaning away from the woman, and she reached a hand out to the edge of the bed, hoping to use that as leverage if she needed to run. "That's why Thomas knew that I was in the woods. You could... smell me."

She nodded. "There aren't many humans foolish enough to go so deep into the woods these days, especially a pair of injured ones."

Carter had been injured too, hadn't he? She had forgotten about that. It felt like a lifetime ago. She wondered if she could get to her feet let alone run from this woman; she didn't even know how long it had been since she stood, but she didn't want to face a werewolf lying in a bed.

"Come now," Leyda said, amusement bubbling

up in her voice. "Is this any way to treat your rescuer? You look at me with such revulsion!"

"My what?"

"Your rescuer, child! Thomas could not have found you without me, as you just admitted. How do you think he would have even known you were in danger? You would have woken only to witness your own flesh being devoured by the werewolves." The candlelight gleamed in her eyes, giving her a predatory appearance, and she chuckled. "You owe me, child."

This gave Mercy pause. She had thought she owed Thomas Farrell, not a werewolf. Perhaps she owed them both. She had never owed someone her life before, other than perhaps her father. This woman, regardless of what she was or what she looked like, had saved her life; and even though Father had told her to survive, Mercy still had his sense of honor in her blood. Even if his honor was flexible at best, Mercy grew up respecting it. A life debt was not something to be cast aside. "Before I agree to anything, I want to know why."

"Excellent." Leyda went over to close the door to the bedroom; again her footsteps didn't make a sound. It was unnerving. At least Mercy understood why. "First you should know how I came here and why I look like this. It's only fair that you should know the full story, given what we're asking of you."

Interesting; so Thomas apparently wanted this,

too, if Leyda was to be believed. That was why he hadn't answered her before. He wanted Leyda to do the dirty work for him.

—————

"YOU CAN'T BE TOO cautious here," Leyda said. "There are ears everywhere, even in a building as locked down as Farrell Mill." She took off the extra fabric that she had unraveled from her face and put it around her throat as she sat down in a chair by her bed. She had strange movements that were somehow human and somehow not at the same time. They made Mercy's hair stand up on end. It was unnatural.

"I assume Thomas told you how he lost his arms?"

Mercy nodded slowly, reaching back through her memory from the tour through the grinders. "Yes, he did."

"So you know that a crazy werewolf crawled her way up the walls of his mill,"—she propped a foot on the wooden edge of the bed—"and tore his limbs from his shoulders with merely her feet?"

Mercy nodded again and tried not to shudder, but she did bring the sheets up to her throat.

Leyda watched her closely. "Did he tell you what happened to the werewolf who dared attack him?"

Mercy had to clear her throat so she could get

the nerve to talk. "He said the guards killed her. He said they shot her to death."

Leyda grinned, and there was something disturbing about the way her teeth shone in the candlelight. Leyda wasn't even transformed, but she still made Mercy's breath catch in her throat when she showed her teeth.

"He didn't kill me. He put me in a cage. That's what Thomas does with things he doesn't understand. That's what he did with you, isn't it?"

Mercy gaped at her. She wanted to protest, but then realized that she had likely been confined to this bedroom for days. Just because it wasn't fitted with bars didn't make it any less of a cage.

"So you did that to him?"

"Yes, I did," Leyda gave a short laugh. "And I don't regret it if that's what you are too afraid to ask. I expected him to kill me. That's what most humans would do in that situation, after I took both of his arms. Not Thomas, though." She folded her arms. "I lived in a cage for days, not sure what he would do with me. It was so tiny, I could barely turn around or lie down. Not unlike the ones you trappers use, I suppose." There was a cold bitterness in her voice.

"So why didn't he kill you?" Mercy asked, trying to tread cautiously.

"He's a fool, one who fancies himself a scientist. In reality, though, he's merely curious... dangerously so. Weeks went by. He had me fed and cared for while he made himself a new pair of arms. I felt like an animal in a zoo, an oddity to be gawked at, a prize to be placed on his mantel and forgotten."

Leyda fetched herself a glass of water and sighed. "Then he did something that surprised me. He came in at his normal time, only this time he came with a chair and a book. It was a children's book, Alice in Wonderland, and he read it to me. He would read a bit then watch me for some kind of reaction. I figured it was merely more of the same. I was just another curiosity for him to unravel. He came every day to see me, and I began to look forward to his company, what little there was of it." She sipped at her glass awkwardly. Her muzzle didn't seem to work well for drinking out of glasses. "Do you know why he did it?"

Mercy thought for a moment, trying to figure out what she would have done in that situation. "I guess he felt bad for you."

The woman gave a wide smile. "That's cute, child. Cute and incorrect. The serum that's used to prevent werewolves like myself from changing back to our human forms also drugs us, as I'm sure you're aware. Did you also know that it's not as effective on the females? It works too well on us. Not only does it rein in our ferocity; it also gives us back our minds. We become trapped inside our beastly bodies but with our minds intact." The ripples in the water glass betrayed her trembling fingers. "Thomas is a dangerously curious man, as I said. He didn't understand the effect the drug had on us, on women. He only understood that we were bad at following orders, like all humans are, I suppose. His serum made my mind human, then he promptly chopped off my arms and shackled me to his mill."

Mercy felt her heart pounding as she tried to wrap her mind around such a horrible fate. It was bad enough to be a werewolf, but she had no idea what she would have done in the same position. With every turn of that grinder, she could imagine her fury rising. Would it have driven her to such a rage that she would climb the walls of her prison without arms just to tear off Thomas's limbs in return? Or would she have merely gone mad? Her eyes settled on Leyda's hands. "But you have arms now. Are they real, or...?"

A bittersweet smile tugged at her lips. "Another of Thomas's gifts." She reached up to her left shoulder and grabbed around as though she had to scratch her back. Instead a plume of steam shot out with a short squeal, then she touched an area on her wrist and her forearm popped open like the lid of an old chest. Inside there were hundreds of tiny gears, moving in every direction. Leyda wiggled her fingers, and inside the gears, pulleys, and levers moved with them. It was the most intricate machine Mercy had ever seen.

"They're not quite the same," Leyda said. "He tweaks mine and gives me new ones every few months. I think he's had his for almost a year now. The guilt, I suppose, eats at him—as it should. I'm one of the fortunate ones." She closed up her arm and nodded out the window. "My brethren not so much. That's where you come in, child."

Mercy felt heat creep up her cheeks. She had been so wrapped up in Leyda's tale that she had forgotten her part in all of this. "The life debt," she whispered. Leyda's gaze was steady. "What do you both want me to do?"

"It may not be apparent to you, but Thomas has tried to cure my curse. Despite his lack of sense at times, he is quite good with chemicals… when the mood strikes him, at least. Thomas read to me, and I found my voice again. He had incredible patience with me as I learned to talk with this." She pointed a finger to her muzzle. "He gave me more treatments, and I lost most of my fur, I lost the bestial crouch, and I learned how to walk upright again. Slowly I became my human self again, more or less." Leyda put her glass aside and turned her gaze on Mercy. There was an intensity to her gaze that made Mercy tremble. "Thomas is working with bits and pieces. He's trying to undo the impossible. What he needs is a complete example. He needs a bigger picture to work from so he can understand how lycanthropy works from beginning to end. He needs to be able to observe the initial transformation and take detailed notes throughout the process. What he needs, my dear child, is a volunteer." She sneered with near glee.

Mercy's pulse pounded in her ears as her headache returned. Her mouth went dry as she struggled to figure out what to even say. There were few things worse than being turned into a mindless werewolf, but willingly having it done had to be one of them. It was the only thing her father would have ever turned on her for, the only thing for which he would have hunted her down. More importantly, her humanity was all she had left. She twisted the sheets in her hands as she fumbled out the words. "What if I refuse?"

Leyda shook her head and laughed. "I had hoped you might be more appreciative of me saving your life, but you're young. I can understand your concern." She set her glass down on the table. "If you don't do this, then I will allow Mitchell and his lackey to kidnap you. I think we both have a good idea what will happen to you then."

Mercy clenched her jaw. "So you know about them."

"Of course I do! Their wretched stench was all over the area where we found you," she snickered. To her this was merely a game.

"I would tell Thomas first! I would tell him that you knew the whole time, too."

Leyda gave a disturbing, toothy grin. "It wouldn't be hard to discredit you, child. A young girl is chased through the woods, and Mitchell is the first person she sees upon waking. You're impressionable, latching on to anyone to blame. Before you said you couldn't remember your attackers' faces, and suddenly you can? It would take hardly any effort on my part." She got to her feet and began wrapping the black fabric around her face again, without a glance to Mercy. "Besides, Thomas and I have a bond; we're both disfigured monsters. What exactly do you have other than that fiery tongue?"

Hot tears threatened to spill, but Mercy pushed them away. "Why are you doing this to me? I've never done anything to you."

"Oh please." Leyda sighed after she secured the fabric again. "This isn't some personal vendetta. You're no victim here, you're just as much to blame as the rest of us. You got yourself into this mess, rather you and your father did. I'm not asking you to die, child, I'm merely asking you to be turned into what I already am. It certainly is the lesser of the two evils." She stared at Mercy for a long moment and reached out to pull her hand into hers. Her skin was warm and soft. If Mercy hadn't just seen the gears inside, she would never have suspected they weren't her real hands. "I know it's difficult for you to understand sacrifice at your age, but think of the good it could do. If this is the last piece of the puzzle that Thomas needs, he could cure all of us. You wouldn't need to be a werewolf for long, and I wouldn't be trapped like this forever. You lose a little of yourself to help hundreds, maybe even thousands."

"You trust him, but why should I? What would he want with a cure?" Mercy asked. "You said he's crazy. Those werewolves out there shackled to the mill are his property, and he has no reason to turn them back. Like you said, people aren't very good at blindly following orders."

"Look at the money he's made from making my kind into docile servants." Leyda gave a sad smile. "Think of what he'll make if he finds a cure, an honest to goodness cure. Think of how this entire town would change because of it. You're probably too young to remember Kanta before it was a werewolf hovel, but I'm not. It used to be a respectable town, a place of innovation and creativity. It used to be important. You could do a lot of good here if you'll simply swallow your pride. All you have to do is allow yourself to be bitten."

Mercy turned away with a huff, pulling her hand free from Leyda. Others might be swayed by all that talk of doing good, of sacrifice, but she had spent most of her life sacrificing for her father. Why did Mercy have to be the one to give up her life and her freedom for others? It wasn't fair. She had already lost her father, why did she have to lose even more?

Leyda narrowed her eyes. "Did it ever occur to you that I'm doing you a favor, giving you the choice at all? I could have bitten you nights ago while you were drugged, and you never would have known."

Mercy gaped at her. She didn't want to believe what Leyda said, but she knew it was true. The thought of owing this woman a life debt as well only made the decision more difficult. She thought of her father lying on the road with a bullet hole through his hand and another through his skull. He had sacrificed everything for her. Yes, he was violent to her. And she didn't agree with everything he believed, but they mostly understood each other. As cruel as he could be, he was the only friend she knew. He was a hard man doing the best he could in a hard world, wasn't he?

She thought of how the trees looked at night when Leyda and Thomas had come for her. She had never really appreciated them before. They had always been a place where danger lurked in the darkness, a place that was restricted for her own safety, a place where the setting sun meant certain death unless prepared. For the first time in ages she allowed herself to ask an impossible question: what if it didn't have to be this way? What if, by helping Leyda and Thomas with this last experiment, they could cure the werewolves for good? She could hear her father's voice in the back of her mind calling her gullible and naïve, but she pushed it back.

A world without werewolves. It would be like lifting a weight off of a limb, and glorious life would flow back into the town again. People would come to Kanta, not for killing werewolves or trafficking its people, but to live and thrive. She would get to see what it had once been like when her mother was alive. Even if her father would think she was naïve, she liked to think her mother would support it. She seemed kind like she would. Just because Mercy and her father hadn't been lucky, that didn't mean others had to suffer as well. If she turned down the offer, Leyda could have her kidnapped or killed. At least this way she had the chance to do some good.

"Why me?" she asked finally. "Why not pick one of those trappers off the street, or one of their sons? Why does it have to be me?"

Leyda sighed. "Those children would be missed."

A hot tear rolled down Mercy's cheek and she gave a bitter laugh. "My mother is dead. And now that my father is too, there's no one to claim me, is that it?" She shot Leyda a hateful glare. "Did you know we would be attacked out there? Did you know they would kill him?"

Caramel eyes stared back emotionless through the slot of black fabric. "If you must know the truth child,"—Leyda leaned in close and Mercy coiled away—"it was your father who brought me here to begin with, and as they wrenched my arms from my body, I vowed that I would see him killed."

"That's not fair," Mercy whispered, shaking from head to toe. "He didn't know. He thought you all were monsters, mindless beasts, he didn't know what it did."

"Does that seem unfair?" Leyda laughed. "This world is unfair, child. You and your father spent your lives enslaving my kind. You should be happy I'm satisfied with seeing only his death. I've been far too lenient with you already. Give me an answer. I need to know if I'm wasting my time talking with you."

Mercy pressed the back of her hand against her mouth. Father had chosen his death years ago, and he didn't even know it. His advice, as much as she valued it, was tainted. Survive for me, he had said, but he didn't know it would entail making a deal with a werewolf. He didn't know that it would involve kidnappers or his old crazy friend. Had he known all of that, he would never have given such advice. She needed to make a decision, on her own, without her father's help, and she needed to do it now; otherwise she could end up dead or enslaved before daylight.

"I'll do it," she said in a hoarse voice.

"Speak up, child. If you truly are volunteering, then you must be forceful about it."

"I said, I'll do it!"

The startled look in Leyda's eyes brought her some small measure of satisfaction at least.

The black-clad woman nodded. "Good. I'll speak with Thomas and make plans for tomorrow. Now that you're well enough to be worth something, Mitchell will soon play his hand. We can't wait much longer." She turned to the door and opened it. Mercy half expected to see Mitchell standing there with a gun, but the hallway was empty.

"Sleep," Leyda ordered. "You'll need your rest for tomorrow."

"I can't sleep. Not after this," she said, wiping her eyes. She wondered if she would ever be able to sleep again.

Leyda turned back to her, and this time her eyes were softer. "Sleep. Once I speak with Thomas, I'll return to watch your door. You won't have to worry about Mitchell tonight, and soon enough you won't have to worry about any of them."

Moving with barely a sound, Leyda left Mercy alone with only the flame of the oil lamp to keep her company. Outside the rain was quieting down again, and the wind howled through the crack from the open windows. It almost sounded like the mournful howl of a werewolf.

Mercy watched the empty doorway for a long time before she sank down into the bed again. She stared out at the darkness, into the storm clouds and listened as thunder rattled the tower. Tears fell from her eyes as she lamented her life, her choices, and her mistakes. She questioned her new alliance with Leyda and Thomas, she questioned her father's morals and knowledge, and as the storm veered off away from Farrell Mill, she wondered what it felt like to be bitten by a werewolf.

That, at least, she would soon know.

9

———————

THE LABORATORY

"YOU SHOULD WAKE."

The words were only slightly more than a whisper, but Mercy jerked awake regardless. For a panic-stricken moment she wasn't sure where she was, but then saw the woman clad in black in the doorway and remembered her promise. Leyda narrowed her eyes and crossed her arms, as if she had been waiting there for some time.

She was here because it was time for Mercy to get bitten. She thought back to the she-wolf that leaped at her in the woods, all glowing eyes and claws. The slash that had gone across her back, the one that could have killed her if she had been a fraction slower. That monstrous form would soon be her fate as well. A pit of fear dropped in her stomach, one that she knew wouldn't leave anytime soon.

"Thomas is coming. He plans to get started

straightaway." Leyda's voice was stern, but there was worry too. Was she concerned something would go wrong? Was she worried about Mitchell?

"Did Mitchell try anything?" She asked, keeping her voice low in case ears were listening like Leyda had warned the night before.

Leyda gave a short shake of her head. Perhaps that was why she was worried. "Get dressed." She motioned to a pile of plain clothes at the foot of the bed. "Be quick about it. I thought you would prefer to be in something other than that disgusting gown." Before Mercy could respond, she stepped out into the hall, pulling the door closed behind her.

Mercy was left alone in the room, bleary eyed and her stomach tied up in knots. Afternoon sunlight streamed in across the floorboards and she could hear the grinders forever turning in the distance. She had seen Leyda the night before, but she must have slept for most of the day. More time lost and wasted laying in bed.

She thought of the werewolves forced to work the grinders in the distance and suddenly recalled her father spitting down on them from the catwalk. She imagined what it would be like if she was one of those werewolves, looking up from that deep pit to see the disgust in her father's eyes. And he would despise her as a werewolf, she had no doubt about that. Tears welled up and she wiped them away with her palm, frustration bubbling up. She didn't have the luxury to cry and regret all the terrible things that had happened to her. She didn't have the ability to wallow in regret and sorrow. She had a job to do, one that she was terrified to do, but one she had agreed to. Her father was many unlikable things, but he was always honorable. He might have been disgusted at her being a werewolf, but he would have been outraged at her backing out of such an agreement. Even if it meant turning into what he hated the most.

She pushed herself gingerly into a seated position. Her side still ached, but she clearly didn't have time to waste. With a shiver, Mercy pulled the gown off, which was damp with sweat, and pulled on the fresh clothes. There was a linen tunic and a pair of loose, linen pants as well. She had to roll the cuffs up on the pants so that they fit.

Her body wasn't ready for so much activity. Just leaning down to her feet, her side ached. Her movements were stiff, but she worked hard not to hurt herself again. She glanced to her old gown on the floor, splotched here and there with bloodstains. She would move past that life, past that pain. She couldn't let pain hold her back, whether it was physical or emotional.

"I'm done," she called.

"Good," Leyda said as she opened the door again and came inside. "Now come along, he'll be here any minute."

Footsteps approached. Leyda took a deep breath. Was it Mitchell, or did she find Thomas that frustrating?

Sure enough, Thomas pushed his way into the room, wearing a coarse white apron that covered his chest and fell down to the floor. It looked like it had old stains that had been through too many washes. To Mercy he looked disturbingly more like a butcher than a mill owner, and she glanced to Leyda with wide eyes. She didn't seem at all phased. Thomas didn't meet her eyes and instead turned to Leyda. "Is she ready?"

Leyda motioned to her. "See for yourself."

He turned to Mercy and gave the largest smile she had ever seen him make. She couldn't suppress a chill of terror at that smile, and she tugged at her tunic.

"You look so much better! Not entirely well, I would say, but good enough."

"The child still looks ill, hopefully she is well enough," Leyda stated.

Thomas waved her off and instead crouched down in front of Mercy. His one eye rolled off to the side as though he couldn't bring himself to look at her directly. Mercy wondered if it was because he too felt guilty about what was to be done to her.

"Are you sure you want to do this?" He asked. "I admit, I'm rather shocked that you would be willing to go through with it, considering all you've been through."

She glanced up to Leyda's gaze: dark, stern, and waiting for her to back down. There was no other option, really. "I'm sure," she muttered.

Thomas's lazy eye rolled back toward her with surprising speed, and Mercy gasped. He loomed closer to her, and she found herself leaning away from him. "Are you certain? I don't want you to regret your decision once the deed is done. Once the change is brought about, there is not a way to turn you back; at least, not at this point."

She gave a quick nod. If she didn't agree to it, she had no doubt Leyda would practically gift her to Mitchell. At least she had some idea of what she was getting into this way. Yes, she would be a she-wolf; yes, she would be a monster; but at least she would have some kind of autonomy, some kind of freedom to call her own. She didn't want to live in a cage for the rest of her life, as a werewolf or otherwise.

"Excellent. Your donation to science will be greatly appreciated," Thomas smiled, putting a hand on her shoulder before climbing to his feet. "Bring her, Leyda"—he turned for the door—"to the lab."

THOMAS PRACTICALLY SKIPPED down the stairwell. It did nothing to help Mercy's already frazzled nerves.

"This will be the final piece, Leyda, the final piece of the puzzle. It has to be. It's the only piece of evidence I don't have at my disposal. In fact, I don't think anyone has actually observed a transformation from start to finish before. Not in a scientific fashion, at least." He gave a short bark of a laugh. "If I dared to tell anyone, no one would believe me, not a single soul! The proof will have to be within the results!"

They walked out into a hallway that opened up to a large circular chamber, the main section of the tower. An open-air, metal, circular staircase emerged off to the side leading downward in the large chamber. Mercy hadn't even noticed they were on the top floor, but now that she looked down the long distance to the ground floor, she felt light-headed. It had to be five floors down.

Leyda appeared beside her, took hold of her hand, and led her to the stairwell. As Leyda took a step onto the metal platform, the entire staircase seemed to rattle. Mercy felt her heart leap into her throat. Leyda had probably intended to lead her down, but instead Mercy was leaning heavily against the woman. She felt weak still, too weak to be taking such a dangerous trip downward. As she began to take in deep breaths, her side began to ache. They had only gone down one floor when she had to put her hand on the railing of the landing and not allow Leyda to pull her to the next set of stairs.

Leyda turned, looking her up and down. Mercy half expected some reproachful comment or a disapproving glare, but instead Leyda gave her a few moments to catch her breath. Thomas trotted on down the next set of stairs, his feet echoing off each metal step in rhythm.

"Imagine… if this actually leads to a cure!" He said with glee.

"A cure," Leyda breathed, looking down at him below. There was such longing in her voice, such desperation—how had Mercy missed that before? "Once we have that, everyone will believe you. Everyone will see the truth." She lifted shaky hand to her cheek. It was hard to tell that her jaw was jutted forward with all the layers of fabric she wore, but Mercy understood. They were so very desperate to find a cure, she wondered if they had considered the experiment might not yield anything at all.

Thomas froze beneath them, peering up at them through the metal grid of the landing. "It shouldn't be too complicated, right?" He glanced to Mercy then back to Leyda. "You don't need to prepare or anything, right? I would hate to get my hopes up and you are unable to… I mean, it won't be too taxing, right?"

Leyda snarled and pulled at Mercy, guiding her down the next flight of stairs. "Don't insult me. If it were difficult, my kind wouldn't be such a threat."

As they came down to his landing, Thomas gave them a boyish grin. It was as if he was talking about building a model train instead of a cure to fight the most deadly blight humanity had ever known. "That's perfect. Precisely what I wanted to hear!"

Mercy put her hand out to catch her breath before going down the next flight of stairs. Leyda grumbled under her breath, but Mercy ignored her. Going down a couple of flights of stairs had never bothered her before. She would do double that just going up to the windmill at her house. Now she got vertigo every time she went down a flight of stairs. Leyda eyed her and tapped her foot, but she allowed for the delay. Mercy felt like she might pass out. Perhaps it was all too much too soon. The more they talked about the transformation, the more her hands shook and her stomach tied up.

"I don't know if I can do this," she said, glancing nervously to Leyda.

"Of course you can!" Thomas bounced down the remaining steps in his telltale rhythm. "You might feel under the weather now, but that will soon be the last of your worries."

Leyda helped her down the last three flights of stairs, but by the final flight Mercy was able to take them on her own. She had to work through the discomfort. Thomas' words didn't exactly help, but they did remind her that what she was feeling was nothing like what was to come. Passing out wasn't going to help, and she was tired of not knowing what was happening to her when she was unconscious. No, she needed to stay on her feet, stay focused, and force her body to get stronger.

Thomas fished a large metal keyring out of his pocket and was sorting through a set of old, iron keys. He smirked as one eye circled up to them as they reached the ground floor. "Considering the level of your injuries, you're actually in quite good condition. Between the pneumonia and the extensive damage to your musculature structure, I'm rather impressed with your status, to be frank."

Mercy was only half listening to him. She was taking deep breaths and taking in the bottom floor of the tower. As she and Leyda moved to the wall where Thomas stood, they were shrouded in shadow. The sound of her breaths and the clinking of metal keys echoed off the metal walls. The afternoon sunlight didn't reach far from the stairwell, and the shadows cast here were dark and angled. The temperature felt like it had gone down, and it took a moment for Mercy's eyes to adjust to the darkness.

She thought Thomas was looking at piping along the wall, but soon she realized there was something more. Three heavy bars sat horizontal along the wall, perfectly spaced from one another, but large enough in diameter to hang tires off of them. The bars locked off an enormous door that filled the entire wall. Mercy watched as Thomas slid a key into a small keyhole and turned it. It was a door, she realized in awe, finally catching her breath.

She didn't like the feel of it. She didn't like the way it hovered in the shadows, or the way it disguised itself from recognition against the piping along the metallic wall. Once the lock was undone, Thomas had to pull the pipes back one by one, using both of his metallic arms. She doubted even her father could have pulled back a single bar on his own.

Bang.

Mercy's teeth rattled as the first bolt echoed up and down the metal stairwell. Everything seemed to shake with that sound, and she wondered if the entire building might collapse with such powerful reverberations.

Bang.

Mercy gripped Leyda's arm. As the echo ran upstairs again, she thought she could hear some-thing scrape on the other side of the door, but discarded it. Sound didn't travel the way it should in this place. Leyda tensed and cocked her head to the side.

"Thomas, you cleaned up, didn't you?"

Bang.

The final latch was pulled back. Mercy backed away from the door and pulled free from Leyda's grip. Something was wrong here. Mercy might not have been the best werewolf hunter apprentice, but she knew when she was being hunted.

———

"THOMAS, you cleaned up, didn't you?" Leyda asked.

"Of course I did," Thomas said as he turned around. "I'm a bit more careful than—" He froze, his fingers gripping the key ring.

Familiar laughter came from behind. Laughter that Mercy hoped she would never have to hear again. She spun around.

From the opposite shadowy side of the stairwell, Mitchell stepped forward, his gun aimed at Thomas. "I think that's good enough, Mr. Farrell. If you would be so kind as to toss the keys over, I might let you live to experiment another day."

Thomas scowled at him, yanking the key from the keyhole. "So the serpent shows his true colors," Thomas snapped. "Honestly, no good can come from killing me. There's very little coin in the main hall, but you could have stolen that at any time. All I really have of value is this place, and you certainly aren't walking off with that."

Mitchell laughed. "You're a crazy, arrogant man, Mr. Farrell, but I'm not here for you. You and your laboratory of horrors don't interest me." His gaze slid to Mercy. "She's worth more than a month of robbing your stores, and I'm not about to let you tarnish her." He glanced to the enormous door. "You and your pet dog just step inside now. I don't need you to go off notifying anyone."

Thomas shook his head. "You're making a big mistake. Do you understand the work you're interfering with? If this works, if this really is the final puzzle piece, a cure to lycanthropy would be worth more than all the money in Kanta. Think, please! I know it's difficult, but do try."

"Get in there!" Mitchell fired a shot upward. The bullet made a series of dings as it ricocheted up the metal stairwell. Mercy fell to a crouch. Mitchell was distracted, his eyes wide as he stared up, as though he had forgotten the entire building was made of metal. Leyda took the advantage. She lunged at Mitchell with her powerful metal arms outstretched in front of her. She landed on him with such force that he fell to the floor. She tore the gun from his grip and broke it into two pieces, then she began to rip Mitchell apart.

Mercy looked away, too horrified to watch as Mitchell's screams echoed up the chamber. As she looked up, she spotted a flash of metal glint in the sunlight from the next floor up. That was when she realized that the laugh she had heard earlier had not belonged to Mitchell at all.

"Leyda, look out!" Mercy screamed. Leyda stiffened, then let out an anguished cry. She put a hand to her side, then dragged herself away from Mitchell's body.

Looking up, Mercy spotted Carter's toothy grin. He held a second dagger between his fingers. "You won't get away from me this time, you little brat. I don't care how much money you're worth!"

Carter's laughter echoed up and down the stairwell. He twisted his body as he flung a second knife, only this time he was aiming for her. Mercy felt a vice-like grip on her arm and was yanked to the side. The knife clattered to the ground only a foot away.

"This is no time to panic," Thomas said as he dragged her to the enormous door. The strength in his grip left no room to object. Behind them she could hear Carter's hurried footsteps as he descended the stairs. Thomas pulled her into the dark room, then pulled the giant door closed behind them. She could hear the locks slide into place on the opposite side. "That should slow him down, but it won't stop him." He struck a match and lit an oil lantern beside the door. Flame flickered down a groove in the wall, lighting other wells along the way, until the long, narrow passageway was completely lit.

This part of the building was nothing like the metallic monstrosity outside. Not only was the corridor disturbingly narrow, but the walls and floor were carved from stone instead of metal. It looked like it used to be a cave before it was converted to a section of the mill. It felt like a crypt, and Mercy put a hand to her throat. At any other time she would never have willingly followed him into this place, but she had little choice now. Already she could hear Carter's cries as he slammed his fists on the door, trying to get in.

Thomas reached down for her arm again, linking his metal fingers around hers, more gentle than he had been before. "We'll go deeper. It'll be safer, I promise."

"Do you have any guns?"

He smirked. "No, but perhaps we can find something useful."

THE CORRIDOR SLOPED DOWNWARD, and the farther they walked, the more distant Carter's banging became. It was colder down here and the scent of lantern oil mixed with a smell Mercy was familiar with: brimstone. It was the scent of werewolf blood, she had smelled it often enough on the werewolf cages when her father brought them back for her to clean, back when she was more an assistant than a full apprentice.

The hall took a sharp turn, and Mercy realized why this area had such powerful protection. The walls were lined with cages, not too different from the ones she and her father had used to ensnare werewolves out in the woods, just larger and likely more expensive. Many of the cages had occupants. Glowing yellow eyes followed them as they crossed to the back of the room. The chamber was large enough so that when the beasts swiped at them, they wouldn't be able to reach them if she and Thomas stayed in the center. That was something else that surprised her: all the werewolves had their arms intact.

"What is this place?" She asked as they moved through the center of the room, her voice echoing off the stone.

"These are the women I've collected. Come, the more aware ones are in the back."

He pulled a long metal rod out of a bushel and handed it to Mercy. It took a moment for her to realize it was a prod stick like the one he had gifted her and her father before.

"Just in case," Thomas said. "Sometimes they can be a bit skittish."

He stepped up to one of the cages. The silver beast within was tall enough to look down on both of them. Thomas twisted the two-handed lock counterclockwise.

Mercy backed away. It was one thing to trust Leyda, a werewolf that clearly had her own mind. Releasing these creatures, though, was practically suicidal. "What are you doing?"

Thomas turned with a grin. "You wanted weaponry, yes? I can think of no better option."

Mercy held up her prod stick. "Can't we use these? Zap him or something?"

"Come now, don't be so cowardly. We'll kill two birds this way." He pulled back the gate, and the metal hinges gave a high-pitched squeal as though in warning. Thomas turned to the silver beast. "Bloody him up as much as you want but keep him alive."

The werewolf snarled and stalked out of its cage slowly. Mercy held up the prod stick, one hand cranking it so that it emitted an electric spark between the metal protrusions at the end. The werewolf looked her up and down, growled, and turned to Thomas. It didn't care about her at all. Its golden eyes were focused only on him. It approached him slowly, and Mercy wondered if he was mistaken. Maybe he had gotten them mixed up somewhere? It didn't look like it had a shred of intelligence. It snarled and bared its knifelike canines, then finally attacked.

It stood fully on its hind legs and towered over

Thomas, snarling and drooling; but Thomas grabbed its forearms. Despite the beast's size and height, he held it fast. Mercy gave a small cry and churned the prod stick faster.

"That's hardly a kind greeting!" Thomas quipped. "Come now, do be civilized, won't you? We don't have time for such foolery."

To Mercy's surprise, the silver beast snorted and lowered down to all fours. Down the hall, they heard the door get pulled open, its massive hinges groaning with the weight. Then came the distinct sound of a gunshot.

Thomas stiffened, and the silver werewolf grew silent. "Move quickly," he whispered. "And be careful. Let me give you a comrade."

He turned to another cell, and to Mercy's surprise there was a much smaller beast inside, one that was only a child. "Join your mother," he whispered. "You're the fastest one here, so if you allow yourself to get shot, I won't ever let you live it down."

The small creature fled the cage quickly and joined up with its mother, who was already waiting around the corner for Carter to appear. Mercy stared in confusion. "How do you know that's her child? They can't talk."

"Trust me," Thomas said as his lazy eye dipped to the floor. "I knew them before they were turned."

"You can't escape me this time, girl!" Carter's

shouts in the tunnel silenced them. "I promise I won't make it easy, either. Nothing quick, you understand? This time you've got no place to run."

Mercy trembled. The electrified prongs in her hands shook, sending sparks up into the air. Thomas grabbed her wrist and Mercy gave a short cry in surprise. He tried to shush her, but it was too late. He pulled her into a corner and had her crouch down behind him.

Carter laughed. The sound made her blood go cold. "Oh, I'm sure you can scream louder than that."

"Don't move," Thomas whispered. "Stay as close to the ground as you can. That pistol was hardly the only gun Mitchell had on him. This could get quite bloody."

She nodded, and Thomas started releasing more werewolves. All the beasts, she realized, were standing up in curiosity; many were snarling and growling, not at Thomas as she would expect, but up toward the hall. They definitely had more intelligence than she gave them credit for.

"Don't kill him," Thomas urged as he released a dark brown beast. "I know it's tempting, but he'll be more useful alive."

Mercy knew precisely when Carter turned the corner, because a peal of gunfire shot across the room. She ducked down to the ground as Thomas had instructed and watched as Thomas unlocked a fourth cage, then got a bullet in the arm. Steam shot out from the limb, and he crumpled inward. The fourth werewolf, a beast as black as midnight, leapt out of its confines and joined its sisters at the far end of the room. It was difficult to tell who was winning, but the gunshots were not diminishing. She had thought that the metal arms that Thomas and Leyda wore were somehow impervious to pain, but that didn't seem to be the case. He was still leaning against the werewolf cage, cradling his arm, and slumping slowly to the ground.

Despite the warnings she'd been given, Mercy discharged the prongs into the stone, then rushed to his side despite seeing stars in her vision from the exertion. Thomas's face was locked in a grimace, and steam spewed forth from multiple places on his arm. He didn't even notice her approach until she touched his shoulder. "What are you doing?" he cried, "It isn't safe!"

"What can I do?" she asked.

He shook his head. "This is beyond you, child." He pushed his back against the bars of the cage as another wave of pain shot through him. More gunfire shot off, and they both jumped. "If I don't get this off, it'll either scald me with steam or explode. It's wiser to keep at a distance."

Through a wide crack in the mechanical forearm she could see gears and tubes bulging. She might not understand mechanical things like the windmill at home completely, but she could learn. "Is it supposed to move like that?"

Thomas glanced down, sweat gleaming on his upper lip. He turned his arm over. "Look for me, Mercy. Do you see a gauge there? It should have a black needle pointing at 200."

She squinted. "I see it, but it's not pointing at 200. It's up to 500 and climbing."

His eyes went wide. He fumbled with the failing limb, but with only one imprecise mechanical hand to work with, he wasn't getting anywhere.

"Tell me what to do," she demanded. "I can follow orders, just tell me!"

"Alright," he breathed. "If you insist." It was easier for him to explain what to do. The pain made him go rigid and his hands were trembling. He told her what pipes to pull, what valves to turn, and what latches to yank. She had just removed the outer casing completely when a scream from across the room sent a chill through her.

She turned to spot the beasts no longer antagonizing and keeping their distance from Carter, but moving in closer. Moving in for the kill. A mangled gun was tossed over one of the werewolf's shoulder as Carter screamed again.

"Don't kill him!" Thomas groaned. "I told them not to kill him."

She turned back to Thomas again, but frowned as a gear popped off his arm. The metal was expanding, growing hot. She could feel the heat on her fingertips, and soon it would get to the point where she wouldn't be able to even touch it without scalding herself. The steam that had been shooting out before had stopped, and she guessed that was a bad sign.

"It's falling apart," she said.

Thomas had his head against the bars of the cage, and she had to shake him to get his attention over Carter's screams.

"Did you hear me? I said it's falling apart!"

His eyes snapped open.

The metal was squealing now as it expanded farther.

"It's too hot!"

He went a shade paler and pursed his lips. "Find a cool part, up here, near me. Then pull. Don't worry about hurting me, just pull as hard as you can. Do you understand me? Once you remove it, throw it. Throw it to the back of the room." He nodded to the farthest end of the laboratory away from Carter and the werewolves.

She nodded and began to pull.

"Be quick," he said with a crazed smile. "Or else our skin will be boiled right off our bones."

Mercy pulled at his upper arm, feeling the pieces come apart like the entrails of an animal. Thomas hitched back against the bars with a groan of pain. Tubing snapped, a metal bracing broke free, and tiny metal threads that she hadn't seen farther in tore loose. Blood dripped with every thread that fell.

Thomas pressed his head against the bars. "Damn," he whimpered. "Oh damn..."

Mercy gave a final tug, and he gave a pathetic gasp. The metal on his fingers had expanded so much that they were now the size of fat sausage links, and they were turning red hot. Even holding the shoulder was almost too hot. She stood and flung the limb as hard as she could toward the back wall.

She knew Thomas had said it was dangerous, and she knew it was under pressure; but she hadn't realized how much damage it could do until it exploded.

A BRIGHT FLASH erupted like a match being lit, only a hundred times brighter. Mercy closed her eyes against it, but then the sound hit her. It was a screeching noise as though the metal had compressed in on itself, tearing itself to shreds. The screech turned to a high-pitched ring that seemed to drown out any other sound. In the distance she thought she heard Thomas say something, but his voice was distant, like he was under water instead of just behind her.

Something hit her, though she wasn't sure what it was. It couldn't just be wind, it felt too powerful to be that, but it knocked her completely off her feet. She was flung several feet to the ground. Everything was shaking, dust fell from the ceiling of the cavern, and then suddenly everything went still again.

Mercy pushed herself up to her elbows before sitting up completely, stars dancing in her vision as she breathed in the scent of smoke and charred metal. Her entire body was shaking, but at least she hadn't had the flesh boiled off her bones like Thomas had told her. Slowly the ringing in her ears faded.

"Mercy," Thomas said, "Mercy, are you alright?"

She felt a hand on her shoulder and turned to see Thomas shaking her. He looked exhausted. She gave a slow nod, trying to calm her racing heartbeat..

"You did an excellent job. If you hadn't gotten rid of it, I hate to think what would have happened." He gave a weak laugh that did little to hide his terror at what had nearly happened to both of them..

It took a moment for her to recalibrate where she was in the room. She looked over to where the arm had hit. A dark black blotch darkened the stone wall, and fragments of the metal arm were strewn about the room like shrapnel confetti.

She turned to the opposite end of the room. There was no sign of the werewolves, but Carter was a bloody mess. She couldn't tell at this distance if he was alive still or not, and she almost didn't want to know. If he was alive, it might make her feel obliged to help him. If she didn't look, she wouldn't have to do anything.

Thomas chuckled. "Those wolves. Aren't they a bunch of cowards?" He put a hand out and helped her to her feet.

"Where are they?"

"They ran to the other side of the wall, up the passage."

"They won't get out, will they? Out to Kanta?"

He shrugged. "It doesn't really matter if they do or not. They know better than to stay out there. I doubt they would make it past the city limits before some trapper got hold of them. They're not fools, they'll be back." It was strange seeing Thomas without an arm. All that was there was the bloody shoulder stump that Leyda had left him.

"Do you think Leyda is alive?"

"I'm sure she's fine. That woman is quite the survivor. Not so unlike you."

Mercy blinked at him.

Thomas crouched down next to Carter and gave a wide smile. "My dear friends obeyed me after all." He patted Carter on the cheek, and the poor man flinched involuntarily.

Mercy frowned at the mess on the floor, at what the werewolves had done to him in such a short amount of time. "He's lost so much blood..."

"Oh, he'll be fine. They've bitten him so many times, he's certain to change. So it seems that you're off the hook then, my dear. Though,"—he sighed—"I'll have to find someone to help me prep him so I can monitor the change as it takes hold. Normally Mitchell would handle it, but..." He chuckled. "I don't suppose you would be interested?"

She stepped forward to take a closer look at Carter. There wasn't a single limb that hadn't been clawed or gnawed on by the werewolves, though they had mostly ignored his vitals. Surprisingly he had survived the attack of three werewolves, four if you counted the child. She couldn't help but smile at the glint of terror in Carter's eyes as he stared up at her, pale and gaunt from the loss of blood, lips trembling, covered in blood from head to toe.

"I'll help," Mercy said. "But only to watch him suffer."

Thomas grinned. "Of course, my dear. I would expect nothing less."

To Be Continued in:
The Blood of Kanta

AFTERWORD

When The She-Wolf of Kanta finally found a home with Aurelia Leo back in 2017, I never imagined that I would revisit this world, let alone expand on this story. I assumed Mercy's story was complete, but I knew deep down that there could be more. I heard from readers how much people loved her and wanted to see more, they wanted to see what happened next. My satisfaction with the ending wavered, and soon I wanted to know how her story continued as well.

Revisiting this book, I got to explore and expand on her life, her background, and her family. I really got to dig into Solomon and Anna's lives, and into the minds of Leyda and Thomas. Continuing Mercy's tale with the Wolves of Kanta series has been so much fun, and I can't wait to share more of her story with you.

Thank you for joining me and Mercy on this journey, and I hope you enjoy where her tale goes next.

Marlena
    August 14, 2021

ALSO BY MARLENA FRANK

The Stolen Series
Young adult, portal fantasy, faeries

Stolen

Broken

Chosen

The Wolves of Kanta Series
Young adult, dark fantasy, steampunk, werewolves

The She-Wolf of Kanta

The Blood of Kanta

The Hunters of Kanta

The Fury of Kanta

The Howl of Kanta

The Colton Fen Series
Weird western, paranormal adventure, werewolves, vampires

Night Feeders

The Man Who Dealt in Death

Monstrous Creatures Series
Young adult, horror, sci-fi, dystopian

The Seeking

Ominous Hour Series

Horror, short stories, standalone

A Beautiful Specimen

Undertow

Standalone

Short stories, horror, dark fantasy

The Impostor and Other Dark Tales

Mystery, film noir, humor, short story

The Mysterious Disappearance of Charlene Kerringer

The Blade Filled with Stars

A kingdom is under siege from a familiar enemy. Families and friends are pitted against each other without reason. Slaughter is imminent while the winged Queen Khafil soars overhead. Desperate and terrified, Anna works with her sister, Lilah, to summon aid from their mother's ancient spell book.

Determined to save their people, the sisters summon Death to help them, but Death is not easily swayed. Neither of the sisters are prepared for the consequences.

Want a peek behind the scenes?
Want to preview my books before they get released?

Get exclusive access to book goodies, giveaways, and cover reveals by joining my mailing list. Not only will you get notified of all my new releases, you'll get an exclusive copy of The Blade Filled with Stars.

Subscribe to the Mailing List at:
http://marlenafrank.com/mailinglist/

ACKNOWLEDGMENTS

This edition of The She-Wolf of Kanta was a journey and a challenge. It had a steep learning curve especially in regards to creating, formatting, and producing my first hardback book. The most difficult step was deciding to turn this novella into something more, to take that first step up the mountain. At first I thought it was impossible.

However the original reviewers wanted to read more from this world. Review after review wanted it to continue, and that impossibility started to fade. I listened to that feedback and slowly found a way for Mercy's story to continue.

This book wouldn't have been possible without my sister, Kelley's, never-ending support. She has always been a sounding board, a sanity check, and a life raft when being an author gets tough. This book and this series wouldn't exist without her help.

A big thank you to my parents, John and Connie, for their continual support and understanding whenever I have to put aside personal time for the author life. Thank you to my Aunt Charmaine for loving Mercy and wanting more of her.

Thank you to my nephew, Patrick, for your patience while I wrote all these words instead of playing Roblox with you.

Next up are my cheerleaders and motivators. Thank you Candace for checking in on me and helping me when I hit a wall. You are always so enthusiastic about writing and publishing and it's infectious! A big thank you to Carla for not only being an incredible cheerleader, but also a constant supporter of my work.

Finally I want to thank my Ko-Fi subscriber, Donna, for supporting me since the very beginning of my book publishing career. Thank you for always being there and always believing in my work. You'll never know how much your support means to me.

ABOUT THE AUTHOR

Marlena Frank is the author of young adult fantasy and horror novels, short stories, novellas, and book series. Many of her books have hit the bestseller charts, including her debut novel, Stolen. Her work has been praised by Readers' Favorite and featured in De Mode of Literature Magazine. Her stories have appeared in anthologies such as Emporium of Superstition, Catstruck!, Heroic Fantasy Quarterly, Georgia Gothic, and The Sirens Call ezine.

Although born in Tennessee, Marlena has spent most of her life in Georgia. She lives with her sister and two spoiled adopted cats. She serves as the Vice President of the Atlanta Chapter of the Horror Writers Association, is an active member of the Science Fiction and Fantasy Writers Association, and is an avid member of the Atlanta cosplay community.

She is also an INFJ, a tea drinker, and a wildlife enthusiast.

Support her on Ko-Fi: <u>ko-fi.com/MarlenaFrank</u>
Follow her at: MarlenaFrank.com